THE SECRET SANCTUARY

T L SHIVELY

Published in the United States by Sanhedralite Editing and Publishing
Edited by: Sherrie Dolby
Cover design by: Karima Creations
Formatting by: Rebecca Poole

ACKNOWLEDGMENTS

I would like to dedicate this book to two of the most important people in my life, my husband and my mom. My mom encouraged my imagination and love of reading from a young age, some of my fondest memories with my mom revolve around a book series about a black cat detective called familiar.

My husband has been one of my biggest cheerleaders not only with my writing but anything I have wanted to do. He always tells me that I can do anything I set my mind to do. Faith like that is hard to come by.

I am very lucky to have them in my life.

GLOSSARY

- Arions - The inhabitants of Sanctuary
- Blood Crystals - The first crystals that were discovered, they were blood-red in color
- Chenra - A magical metal used by Serdita and her sister Soliel to make music
- Command Center - The military establishment that resides in the mountains that protects Sanctuary
- Crim - Crystals used to enhance the power of an Arion, only the Guardians are able to use their powers without a Crim
- Crystal Essence - The powder from crystals that is highly unstable
- Healers - Arions who use the crystals to heal or do damage control such as adjust someone's memory
- Illusion Crystals - Crystals used to create illusions to help the Arions keep the knowledge of their existence from the world
- Leaders - A group that run the Sanctuary, it should be noted that Arions have never seen any of them

- Magine - A shadow creature created by the Shadow Master, Crims don't affect this creature, only the Guardians can stop it
- Memory Crims - Crystals used in altering someone's memory
- Mythrian Metal - A special metal used in the creation of Crims
- Normies - Mortals who know nothing of the Sanctuary
- Parent Crystals - Large Crystals that are used to give the crystal Crims their power
- Power Ball - A crystal ball used in training one's powers
- Productive Crims - Crystals used in daily life around the Command Center powering computers, opening doors and more
- Rotary - The magical Crim bracelet that was designanted as unstable but now resides on Telara's wrist
- Shadow Generals - More human looking than the minions and bigger in size, they command the minions and only battle when needed by the shadow master
- Shadow Master - The being that controls all the shadows
- Shadow Minions - The lowest ranking of Shadows and also most common, if you were playing chess these would be considered the pawns
- Shadows - Creatures made of shadows commanded by the Shadow Master
- Stargazer - A black slim box resembling a small

laptop covered with strange symbols that only I.Q. is able to understand

- Static Room - Room in the Bungalow where the Guardians could relax with their powers

BRIGHT EYES TRANSLATIONS

- iremisoume ligo pyrotechnima mou = calm down my little firecracker
- katharisete to myalo sas pyrotechnima = clear your mind firecracker
- den eiste etoimoi na fainetai = you are not ready it seems
- fotia miza = fire starter
- I mitera fysi = mother nature
- Aioliki peripatitis = wind walker
- Exaerosis nerou = water breather
- Pago michani = ice maker
- Astrapi epithetikos = lightning striker
- Myalo Klinon = mind bender
- Erchontai = come
- Ela mazi mou = come with me
- Tin katapolemisi tis pyrotechnima skotadi = fight the darkness firecracker
- Oti ena koritsi = that a girl
- Tora antepitethoun = now fight back

- Chrisimopoilsei ti dynami sas = use your power
- To gegonos afto mas odigei pouthena = this is getting us nowhere
- Ochi = no
- Daneizetai tin exousia = borrow the power
- Evge = well done

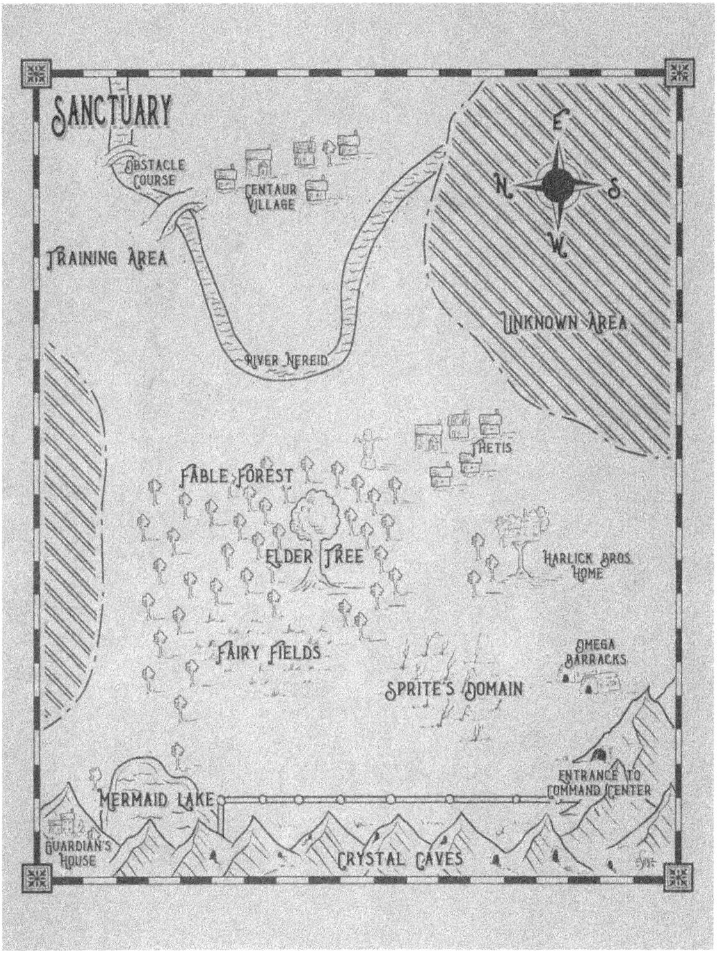

SANCTUARY
OBSTACLE COURSE
CENTAUR VILLAGE
TRAINING AREA
RIVER NEREID
UNKNOWN AREA
E
N
S
W
THETIS
FABLE FOREST
ELDER TREE
HARLICK BROS. HOME
FAIRY FIELDS
OMEGA BARRACKS
SPRITE'S DOMAIN
ENTRANCE TO COMMAND CENTER
MERMAID LAKE
GUARDIAN'S HOUSE
CRYSTAL CAVES

THE DRAGON WAKES

The dark-haired gentleman sat behind his oak desk, shuffling through the stacks of paper on top of his desk in search of his objective when something on his bookshelf caught his eye. He stared at the tallest bookshelf in his office, as if frozen in place. He stood up and walked over, wondering if he was seeing things. There sat two dragon statues, each with a crystal sphere floating just above their outstretched claws. The only difference between the two was the color; one was black onyx while the other was white marble. Just as he was about to turn back around, the white dragon opened its eyes, and the sphere glowed brightly.

"So, it has begun."

1
———

"FAIRIES."

Telara Lee Christos was standing at the window of a room in the Bungalow watching a fairy flying outside. She and her friends were waiting for Lucius, the Caretaker of Sanctuary. They had won a scholarship for a once-in-a-lifetime adventure at Sanctuary where dreams come true. It was advertised as a summer camp for teenagers. She was sure it stated on their on-line site that their program was ranked the highest for physical fitness and creativeness in the nation.

Telara looked back into the room at her friends; she and Tia had known each other from the cradle. Their mothers were best of friends, and their daughters happened to be born on the same day and time. The others they had met on the first day of Kindergarten. Vanna, the quiet one, was playing by herself at one of the puzzle tables. I.Q. (whose real name was Max), the genius of the group, was teaching the teacher how to access her new email. Cole, the ladies' man, was showing off his new shades to anyone who would pay attention, although they got confiscated by naptime. Chad, the sci-fi fanatic and class clown, was trying to put as many straws up his nose as he could fit. And finally, there was his twin brother, Chance, the athlete of the bunch, who was handing his brother the straws. To this day, they were not sure what brought this motley bunch together; but, by the end of the day, they were all best of friends and had remained so through their childhoods.

They believed they were here for a summer camp experience that would make them envied by their peers.

Some summer camp. Spending a week running through an obstacle course any military drill sergeant would drool over and being yelled at by a centaur as they stumbled and fell from the flying projectiles from all around. Yeah, this is how we envisioned spending our summer vacation. And there are still seven more weeks left, Telara thought as she leaned her head back against the seat of the very comfortable, pristine, white couch that matched the other furniture in the room.

The furniture was all white, without a single stain or tear, and the tables were all glass with what looked like crystal legs. This was the one room in their new home in which she really hated being. She was afraid of leaving fingerprints on the table tops or that dirt from her pants would leave a smudge on the furniture. It was definitely different than her parents' home with wooden tables and multi-colored furniture and the western theme that her mother seemed to love. She would rather be in the common room where the chairs were still white but made of vinyl so they were easier to clean if something spilled.

Wonder what would happen if something actually spilled on any of the furniture in here? Telara thought.

As soon as she thought that, her glass of grape juice sitting on the table beside her started to wobble, and then tipped over to spill a nice, deep-purple puddle on the cushion next to her. She jumped up, ready to go find a cloth to soak up the juice before it could set in; however, to her amazement, the couch seemed to absorb the liquid until there was no trace of any of the juice left. She looked over at the others and saw they were also watching the disappearing stain. They looked at one another without saying a word, and then turned back to what they were doing previously, as if they had not just seen the juice magically disappear.

Just another entry into my journal about the weirdness of this place.

She turned back to the tiny blue fairy who was flying from flower to flower, reminding her of the humming-birds back at home in her mother's garden. This fairy, the one they called Flash due to how she could fly fast enough to make her wings look like nothing but a flash of light, was only one of the amazing creatures that they discovered here.

Telara shook her head as if trying to clear her mind, causing a lock of her blond hair to fall down over her eyes. She combed her fingers through her hair, effectively pulling the lock of hair out of her vision. Looking back at Flash, she thought about what all their classmates back home would say if they told them all they had seen in just one week here at Sanctuary. Starz and Starla, the flower-power twins, would of course believe them without a doubt. Those two have always been ones to believe in the unbelievable. Ciara would want to know if they had brought a fairy home as a pet, probably asking if she could also have one. Telara chuckled to herself thinking Flash's reaction if told about that; the little fairy would probably put spiders in their beds for a week. Telara shuddered at the thought; spiders happened to be her biggest weakness. Flash was nice, but she had some of her sprite cousin's trickster tendencies. Sprites were well-known for their mischief, although they had not seen any of those yet to be able to compare. Everyone else would just laugh and tell them, "Good one," as if they were all pulling a practical joke. That was Cole and Chad's specialty, so Telara had to admit she wouldn't blame them for feeling that way.

Telara grimaced as she realized that out of all their friends at home, the three most eccentric of their friends would be the only ones to believe them. Then there was Raven, who would use the information as ammo against them in any way she could. *Heck, she would probably have the white men in coats come to collect us.* Telara's thoughts went dark as she thought of Raven; she couldn't remember what had happened to start that feud. All she knew was they hated one another. Raven and her clones always went out of their way to give Telara and her friends trouble.

Thinking about home had her thinking of her twin sister Tiara. They were completely identical. Her and Tia may resemble each other with their long blond hair, Telara's more straight than Tia's long wavy locks, and of course their blue eyes that were very similar except that Tia's was more of a gray blue while Telara's was a deep sea blue along with her sister's, but Telara and Tiara were identical down to that one little freckle they both had on their right knees. However, that was where the similarities between the two stopped. They had different friends, different goals, and different personalities. She was sure if she wrote home to tell her sister of all that she had seen, Tiara would just claim that Telara was trying to prank her. They weren't as close as most twins, but they did love each other, in their own way.

Now, they were living in a world that belonged between

the pages of a fairy tale. After a week here at Sanctuary, there wasn't much she wouldn't believe now.

Sanctuary, Telara thought, shaking her head trying to wrap her mind around it all. *They definitely picked the wrong name for this place. Should have been more like Whacky World.*

Tia was sitting on a white ottoman with her legs crossed, although Telara noticed her sending furtive glances over to the couch, watching Cole and Chad. They had brought with them their many decks of cards and were now in the process of creating their largest house of cards yet. Vanna was standing back, camera in hand, snapping pics to document the feat for them. Chance, Chad's twin brother, was watching them with interest. They always seemed to want to go bigger and better, so their house of cards would never be able to be finished before it toppled. I.Q. was sitting on the window seat by Telara, watching Flash flit around outside the window. Telara watched I.Q., the brainy one of the bunch, who always had a scientific reason for any super-natural discovery, and wondered exactly how his scientific mind was processing the past week. At first, he kept saying there were people who were dressing the part, but it was hard to keep saying that when their drill sergeant, as they had come to call Raphael, had the head and torso of a man but the body of a horse.

"*Centaur,*" Telara corrected herself. She was sure Raphael would demand 50 laps around the obstacle course for that slip up.

I.Q. didn't mess with Raphael to try to prove he was correct. Instead, he decided to prove the fairies were anima-tronics and held up by wires. He had three different fairies pulling his hair in different directions before they could get them off of him. He still had a small scar above his right eye from the skirmish. After that, I.Q. kept his scientific views to mutterings whenever they came across a new mythical discovery.

Mythical discovery.

Telara looked back out the window and realized Flash was gone, probably going to harass one of the satyrs, as that was one of Flash's favorite past-times. She would find a satyr that had managed to sneak up on a nymph and then fly down making crowing sounds, frightening the nymph off. Flash had found herself in a fairy trap more times than not by some very irate satyr.

This place was full of Greek mythology and so much more with its centaurs. *Well centaur,* Telara corrected herself as she had only seen one in the week here. She seemed to be correcting herself a lot lately. There were also nymphs, gnomes, satyrs, fairies, and even mermaids.

And those were just the ones we have seen so far; I wonder how many more creatures there are here that we haven't seen.

The only other human that they had encountered since being here was Lucius. He had greeted them as they got off the plane before being herded into the limo where not only could you not see into it, but you could also not see outside it. They were later informed this was to keep Sanctuary protected from outsiders; they didn't understand why until they discovered many of the inhabitants here.

Their days were spent with Raphael over at the training field. Training consisted of an obstacle course that was as brutal as it was treacherous. Chad had made many complaints that this had to be a violation of some code, to which his brother told him to go ahead and lodge his complaints with the nearest mythical law enforcement. Daily hand-to-hand combat left them sore and frustrated, and they spent more time on the ground after a sweep from Raphael's staff than not. There was the crystal ball that was the cause of the bruise Telara was absently rubbing on her shoulder, thanks to Cole. Raphael insisted they spend the last hour of the day playing catch with the heavy ball, although none of them could figure out what the purpose was.

It was supposed to be a great honor to be chosen to come to Sanctuary to learn more about themselves. Telara had yet to learn anything that didn't either confuse the hell out of her or cause her more aches and pains. Lucius, the reason they spent every night exhausted and the reason they were all gathered together now, was supposed to meet the group here to explain what was expected of them.

Because, of course, he couldn't do that our first day, Telara thought sarcastically.

She thought about how, during their first meeting, he called her the leader of the group. She had informed him they didn't need a leader; they were friends, not some sort of gang. She had thought it was just a passing comment but after this week, she wondered if there was more to it than that.

"You okay?"

Tia had also watched the stain disappear as if it was sucked right into the cushion with no trace. The things they had seen since they came to stay here would fit right into a fiction book or movie. Chad, their sci-fi fanatic, insisted this was a colony of aliens that had come to Earth to study humans.

"Telly?" Tia brought her out of her reverie.

"Isn't any of this creeping you out?" Telara finally asked the question they had all been avoiding this whole week.

Tia sighed deeply. She sat next to Telara, crossing her legs.

"Of course it is. I think it is creeping all of us out." As she said it, she looked at the others who were nodding their heads in agreement. Telara looked over at Chad in amazement; after all, he was the one who seemed to be gushing like a kid at Christmastime.

Chad laughed at her look. "Don't get me wrong, Tel. I think it is cool as can be but still, yeah, I'm a bit creeped out. I mean watching it on T.V., or even reading it in a book, you would think it would be awesome to actually be on another planet or even chasing after a nymph through the woods." He grinned over at Cole while saying the last part. Then, he turned back to Telara all serious. "But to actually see a mermaid swimming in the lake and then just disappear as if she was never there… The pond is not that big, and Chance dove in and didn't see anything."

"I never did touch bottom," Chance interjected. "Raphael came hollering for us before I could."

Chad and Chance were completely identical and while the group had no problem telling them apart, probably because of how different their personalities were, not everyone else was able to tell the brothers apart. Both were tall and slender with slightly wavy brown hair and hazel eyes that had many girls back home swooning over them. The one time everyone could tell them apart was during swim season when Chance would shave his head for the meets. He said it made him swim faster. Chad, who was considered the class clown, would then start calling him Lex Luther.

"Yeah! And if that isn't suspicious itself… That guy always seems to pop up right before we can do any investigating into the things we see," Cole said in disgust. "When you and Van went into the woods after the goat-man you saw, he showed up. '*Back to the field,*'" Cole said in an attempt to impersonate their teacher, for want of a better word, this past week. "*No goofing off.*"

Everyone chuckled. Raphael did seem to have eyes in the

back of his head; either that, or one heck of a sixth sense. Whenever they veered from the path he had them on, he would come from out of nowhere to herd them right back to where he wanted them with his gruff voice and brusque manner. It also was rather irritating and gave them many grumblings whenever he was out of earshot. It wasn't like he was a bad guy or anything; but sometimes it seemed as if he were watching them closely, looking for something more. More of what, they didn't know. It was just a feeling she had.

Besides the obstacle course, hand-to-hand combat, and the stupid crystal ball training they had with Raphael, he would also have them train with some wooden dummies. Chad called them the "Chucky Dolls;" he swore they were possessed and very much alive. The others chuckled about it at first but, as time wore on, they had all started to wonder. There was one Tia always seemed to get stuck with, and it seemed like it was definitely jerking her chain. The object of the dummy training was to jump and do a round-house kick to the head of the dummy. It took them the first part of the week to be able to manage the move without the dummies. The next move was to work with the dummies and connect their foot with the side of the dummy's head.

"The stupid thing keeps moving," Tia groused during training the other day.

After the sixth attempt, and her having to pick herself up from the ground while brushing off the dirt, Telara could see the frustration on her face. What happened next, none of them expected. Tia threw out her arms.

"ARRGGHHHHH!"

WHOOSH!

It was midday, and there was no wind blowing yet, but a very strong gust of wind came out of nowhere and knocked the dummy right over. They had stopped their training to look at the dummy, and then to Raphael, expecting him to yell at them for not doing it right.

Rafael didn't acknowledge the wind or the dummy now lying down on its side. "Training's over; go back to your quarters."

They looked at each other briefly before nodding to Rafael, and then they beat a hasty trail back to their quarters.

Their quarters were built into the side of the mountain that loomed over the valley where they trained. While the valley itself reminded them of summer camp, the building their quarters were in made them think of a fairy tale that meets a sci-fi novel. The furniture and appliances in the building would make any movie set designer jealous; yet, it also had the rustic look of fairy tales. They called their new home "The Bungalow." Vanna thought calling it a bungalow would make it feel more like a vacation than boot camp.

But rather than heading back to the bungalow, they went to sit by the lake to talk about their day and the freak gust of wind. Chad's theory was Tia was a wind witch and caused the wind due to her frustration with the dummy. They argued over it for a good hour, except for Chance, who kept watching the lake where they could have sworn they saw the mermaid the day before. They looked at the water and remembered when Chad had pushed Cole in so he could go and check out the red-haired mermaid. They chuckled as they remembered Cole getting out of the water dripping wet.

Cole had stalked up to Chad. Everyone swore he was so mad you could see the steam rolling off him in waves, his sandy brown hair drying quickly and curling at the nape of his neck. Cole's normally chocolate brown eyes looked almost black in his anger, although Vanna swore she saw some red flecks that resembled flames dancing in them. He stood eye-to-eye with Chad even though Chad still wasn't even paying attention to him. Chad's attention was on the red head who had disappeared beneath the waves yet again. Cole wasn't as slim as Chad and Chance, but they were all around the same height. Tia moved herself between them before anything could start, although being several inches below their 6ft height she wasn't much of a deterrent.

Those were only a few of the incidents having no explanation; even I.Q. couldn't find any. There was also the microwave oven that exploded on them after I.Q. slapped it when it wouldn't turn off. The plants in Vanna's room were growing so much she had to bring them outside and plant them in the ground. They had grown right out of the planters. No matter what food Chad decided to eat, it would always end up cold, even the soup he warmed up in the microwave. Yet, Cole seemed the exact opposite: a pop he grabbed from the fridge that was cold at first become lukewarm within minutes.

The only one who didn't have anything strange happen to her was Telara. *Well, until today,* Telara thought, staring down at the milky white cushion. She could have sworn the shapes on her bedroom ceiling the other night had moved but after staring at them for several more minutes, she figured she must have been seeing things. *Maybe not.* She grimaced.

"So, have any of you told anyone back home about any of this?" Telara asked her friends.

"Yeah. Hey mom! This place is cool, but you know what? I think there's a mermaid in the lake, and hey, guess what? Tia can shoot air out of her hands!" Chad said chuckling. "I think I would be going home to some guys with a nice white jacket that has my name on it."

"Actually, mom would just laugh and figure you were

trying to pull a Lark on her," Chance chuckled. And with Chad's track record, no one argued.

"Probably," Chad conceded. "The point is, though, who would believe us?"

Tia picked up one of the couch cushions and smacked Chad upside the head, her long hair whipping with her as she did.

"What?"

"I did not shoot wind from my hands," Tia told him frowning.

"Well then you explain where the wind came from."

"I don't know, but it wasn't me."

"On the contrary, my dear, the wind did indeed come from you," a smooth voice said from behind them.

2

THERE, in the doorway, stood the man who Telara was thinking about moments before: Lucius. He wasn't very young, but he couldn't have been more than 40 years old. His hair, while very much black in color, had a few streaks of gray throughout.

Actually kinda makes him look distinguished, Telara thought, thinking of her dad's favorite expression, "Men don't grow old, they just get more distinguished," which usually started her parents' favorite mock argument about who was older.

Lucius was wearing jeans and a button-down shirt with the sleeves rolled up to under his elbows. Quite a contrast to the dark black suit he wore when picking them up. This look seemed to suit him much better in Telara's opinion.

"Well, do I pass?"

The question brought Telara and the others out of their musings. Telara looked up into Lucius's face and realized he was watching them with something akin to amusement. He smiled at them and then walked into the room as if he owned the place, which, to be fair, he did run it. She looked into his eyes and could not contain the gasp that left her lips. At first glance, his eyes looked deep blue but when you looked right into them, it was as if they were blue ice. Telara had never really paid much attention to Lucius's eyes before but, then again, they were more awed by the place in the beginning and too tired to notice much after their training had started. When he raised his dark eyebrows at her, she realized she was staring again.

"Ummm, I guess," Telara mumbled, looking anywhere but those very intense eyes.

His eyes seemed a contrast to the rest of him, with his serene smile and the laid-back attitude he always seemed to have. Telara wondered if there was anything that could shake up his calm demeanor.

"So you wanted to see us?" she asked when it became apparent no one else was going to.

Lucius chuckled and asked them, "Have you been enjoying your stay here at Sanctuary?"

Telara stared at him, a bit slack-jawed. Lucius asked the question as if they were vacationing at the nearest Holiday Inn.

"Well….gee….if you count seeing creatures that apparently jumped out of the pages of many different fairy tales, yeah, we are having the time of our lives," Telara replied, her voice dripping with sarcasm.

Sarcasm that rolled right off of Lucius since he calmly replied, "Good. You have met some of your neighbors then."

Telara looked at him in total disbelief. He was acting as if seeing centaurs, fairies, and mermaids were normal.

Of course, here in Sanctuary, I guess it is normal.

They went quiet, not exactly sure what to say next. They had many questions running around in their heads but were not sure how exactly to ask them without feeling like an idiot.

All they had seen looked and felt so real, but everything they had ever been taught told them it couldn't be true. Telara couldn't even imagine what was going through I.Q.'s mind at this point.

"Yes, we have met our so-called neighbors," I.Q. said, causing them to look at him, very interested to hear what he had to say. "But why are they even here?"

"This is their home."

"No, I mean why do they even exist?" he asked with great exasperation, running his hands through his dark locks. His hair looked as if he had just gotten off of a roller coaster: ruffled and messy, Although that wasn't uncommon for I.Q. When he was dealing with something that made him have to think harder than usual, his hands would make short work of any neat hairstyle his brush had done that morning.

Telara could feel I.Q.'s frustration not only with the situation but also with Lucius's calm attitude towards something that was causing them many troubled thoughts.

"Why does a rock exist?"

"You know what I mean!" I.Q. almost yelled at Lucius's still smiling face.

"I'm afraid I do not."

"They are fairy tale creatures that are not supposed to exist, so why do they? Or are they as fake as the reason we're here?"

Telara was surprised by the venomous tone in I.Q.'s voice, as were the rest. He had always been the unflappable one who could keep his head during any confrontation. But, then again, this was his first one with such an opponent as Lucius.

"The creatures inhabiting Sanctuary are as real as your reasons for being here," Lucius told them, and then he turned to look directly at Tia. "As real as the gust of wind your friend here created."

"What do you mean? The wind I created?" Tia interrupted while staring at Lucius, refusing to look away. "I can't do anything like that."

"Really?" Lucius asked. "And how many times have you tried?"

"W-well, none," Tia slowly said. "But why would I?"

"Indeed, why would you?"

"So, wait a minute," Chad said. "You're trying to tell us Tia has some sort of supernatural power?"

"Yes, and she is not the only one." He smiled at them.

They looked at one another, not sure what to say. Tia looked down at her hands and then back to Telara, who was also staring. Telara looked over at Lucius, who, after making that one statement, continued to smile serenely at them. They waited for what seemed like several minutes before Telara could no longer take the silence.

"Why are we here? And please don't try to tell us this is a normal summer camp."

"You're here because of your ancestry."

"Our ancestry?" Telara was not the only one confused by the statement. Not if the confused expressions on her friends' faces were anything to go by.

Lucius smiled. "Yes, one of your ancestors was a child of a god or goddess."

The room went very quiet for several minutes after the bombshell Lucius dropped on them. Telara stood up and walked briskly over to the other side of the room to put as much space as she could between Lucius and herself. Tia was still staring down at her hands with a zoned-out expression. Vanna had her arms around Tia, but even her expression was a bit phased out. Cole, Chad, and Chance were staring at the house of cards as if the answer to all this madness was hiding behind one of them. I.Q. stood up and started picking up crystal figurines and a lamp on one of the tables.

"You want us to believe that we are descendants of gods?" Telara could not believe what she was hearing.

"I know this is a bit of a shock," Lucius began, only to be interrupted by Telara, who was still across the room but now pacing back and forth.

"A bit of a shock?" she asked incredulously. "First, you want us to believe all the creatures we have seen here are real rather than animatronic, then you want us to believe we carry the blood of gods? What's next? Gonna tell us we are mankind's last hope for salvation? We are just normal teenagers who mistakenly thought they had won a trip to what was supposed to be the most sought-after summer camp for teens. Instead, we find a place run by someone who should have been taken away in a white coat long ago." Telara stopped to take a breath after her tirade and stared at Lucius, who was watching I.Q. move a picture frame on the wall rather than paying attention to anything she had said. Seeing this, she grew angry at this whole situation. "Did you hear a thing I said?" she asked him through gritted teeth.

Lucius turned back to her with a serene smile on his face that made Telara grind her teeth even more. "Yes, I heard everything you said. I believe half of Sanctuary was able to hear what you said. Your voice tends to carry, and you were quite loud."

Telara choked down a scream at his calm manner and voice. *How dare he sit there all calm and unsettled while our whole world feels as if it is falling completely apart?* Telara's hands curled into fists as she fought the urge to slap that perfect pristine smile right off his face. Her parents had warned her many times about her temper, and she didn't think getting sent home for harming the director, or whatever he was, would sit well with her parents.

"Did you honestly believe all the inhabitants you have met during your time here so far were animatronic?" he asked, seeming to be very interested in her answer.

I.Q.'s wanderings now had him trying to remove the crystal fixtures on the wall, but Lucius paid him no mind as he waited for Telara's answer.

"Well..." Telara started to say but stopped as she was not sure exactly how to put her thoughts into words. They seemed to think all the creatures they had seen were animatronic but, after a week of seeing them more often, they had started to get doubts. There was no way Telara was going to admit it to him, though. Before she could come up with anything that would sound good, Lucius gave a satisfied smile and leaned against the wall.

"I thought not." Before Telara could contradict him, he looked at I.Q. who was still messing with the crystals on the wall. "And exactly what are you looking for, young man?"

"I'm trying to locate the cameras," I.Q. informed him still trying to get the crystal off the wall.

"I can promise you there are no cameras here," Lucius said, and then he walked over to the doorway. "Why don't we take a walk, and you can let me introduce you to some of your neighbors so you can meet them up close? Then, afterward, if you are still interested, I will answer any questions you have."

"And if we aren't?" Telara asked him.

"Let's cross that bridge when we come to it, shall we?"

They left the bungalow but, rather than lead them down the trail to Raphael's training area, he veered off to the right. He told them the lake next to the bungalow was named Mermaid Lake. There, they were finally able to meet the red-haired Bromhilda, the beautiful mermaid they had seen from before. Brom, as she told them to call her, introduced them to her two sisters, Celeste and Sura. They left as Brom and her sisters started a splashing war. They ended up a little damp, except for Chance.

Next was Fairy Fields, called such because the plants and flowers in the field were home to the resident fairies. Some also made their homes in the smaller group of trees lining the edge of Fairy Fields. It was in the trees where they saw Flash with a few of her friends, who were giving I.Q. very dirty looks.

"Hey I.Q., looks like your little buddies remember you," Cole chuckled.

Tia glared at Cole. "Ignore him I.Q. He is an idiot."

"Hey, I was just funning. I.Q. knows that. I don't mean any harm." Cole put his arm around I.Q., who shrugged it off. "You know that, don't ya, Bud?"

I.Q. shook his head and kept an eye on Flash, who had perched on Lucius's shoulder. Lucius introduced her to them as Lucy. It seemed her family and friends were not as interested in them as Flash was, or maybe the memory of I.Q. grabbing them by their wings was still fresh in their minds. I.Q. absently rubbed the scar above his eye that he had received from that fateful endeavor.

"Fairies are very private by nature," Lucius explained then motioned toward Flash/Lucy who was still perched on his shoulder. "Although some are ruled more by curiosity rather than caution." Flash/Lucy grinned at them a very bright smile.

When Flash discovered their nickname for her, due to Chad slipping up, she insisted on being called Flash from that moment on.

Next, they walked by a humongous tree that stood higher

than most buildings in New York. Vanna had referenced it to the Statue of Liberty upon first seeing it, saying it looked very majestic and larger than any tree she had ever seen. Lucius told them this was called the Elder Tree. Its age was unknown, but most called it timeless. Beyond the Elder Tree was the Fable Forest, with its lush green shrubbery and many different species and colors of flora that decorated the forest floor. Lucius didn't take them into the forest but kept walking.

They met some woodland nymphs who were playing in the trees. One brown-haired, golden-eyed nymph introduced herself as Elma before giggling and disappearing into the forest.

"What was the smile about?" Cole asked, glancing at the spot where Elma had disappeared. Upon getting no answer, they decided to catch back up with Lucius, who had not stayed to see the smile. Before they could take another step, they fell forward. Looking down at their feet, they saw little tiny roots had intertwined with the laces on their shoes and sandals.

Lucius came back to help them out of their predicament and, while they saw no evidence of amusement on his face, Telara was sure she saw his eyes twinkle.

He probably knew what was going to happen, Telara thought angrily.

She supposed she should be looking at this as a great adventure. After all, how many people can say they have met real-life fairies, mermaids, and prank pulling nymphs? Looking at her friends, who were grinning at their predicament, she tried to be upbeat as well. But the fact they were all lied to about this place, and the fact that it had taken Lucius one full week to try to explain it to them, did not sit very well. She wished she and her friends could talk to each other about what was going on without anyone overhearing but, right now, it wasn't possible. They would have to wait until later. The looks on their faces kept changing; one minute it would be confused, then intrigued with some other emotions thrown in, and then back to confused. Of course, right now, it was complete amusement at Elma's little prank.

They passed the River Nereid that ran under the obstacle course with which they had gotten pretty familiar with this past week. There, they saw several water nymphs playing in the water. The nymphs paused in their antics to watch them walk by. After Elma, they decided to keep their distance and were careful to watch where they walked.

When they reached the training area, Raphael was nowhere to be found.

They climbed up on a picnic table and sat there, not sure exactly what they were supposed to do or say at this point. It was kind of hard to dispute all they had seen as real. Telara had to admit to herself she was starting to believe it before the tour and now...

I still won't give Lucius the satisfaction of hearing me say it loud though.

I.Q. had his head in his hands, looking a bit under the weather. Telara felt bad for him, knowing how this must be very conflicting for him.

"So, Sanctuary isn't what we were led to believe it was?" Vanna asked very quietly, not looking at anyone in particular.

Lucius smiled as you would towards a child you were trying not to frighten. "Sanctuary is indeed a summer camp of sorts." Lucius smiled at their looks of disbelief. "It is just a bit more than an average summer camp. Here you will learn more about yourself than you thought possible."

"That we are related to either a god or goddess," Telara

supplied for him, wearing her best condescending smile. She couldn't explain why she was acting the way she was, and she knew it was being downright rude, but she couldn't help herself. Things were happening that she couldn't control, and she didn't like it.

Rather than rising to the bait, Lucius nodded to Telara in agreement and said, "Yes, those related to gods and goddesses and then there are some who happen to be associated with Sanctuary in other ways." He held up his hand when it seemed like they were going to question his last comment. "But we are here to talk about you and not the others; that will come in time. So, why don't you tell me how your past week has been?"

"Besides feeling as if we stepped into the pages of a fairy tale/sci-fi book cross over? More confused than anything, and I can safely say that is what we all feel." Telara held out her hands gesturing to her friends, who were silently watching them both. She ignored Lucius's raised eyebrows at her last comment. "We thought we had signed up for a summer camp more spectacular than any summer camp out there. This was supposed to be the summer camp everyone wanted to go to, and it was supposed to be an honor to go to." The memory of Raven getting highly irritated they had all won the trip instead of her and her clones was enough to make Telara smile just a bit. It was the one thing Raven's "daddy" couldn't buy for her.

"You don't agree with that?" Lucius, who had been listening very intently, asked.

Telara shrugged. "In all honesty, we don't know. This is definitely not what the website says it is. There are no fairies or any drill sergeant centaur pictured there."

"Agreed. But as I told you, the fairies are pretty private

people and Raphael…well, let's just say he is not one for getting his picture taken."

Cole and Chad chuckled. Telara ignored them and instead stared at Lucius.

"So, why is there nothing that tells us exactly what you do?" Telara asked. Even though she was sure she knew, she wanted to hear him say it.

Lucius chuckled "Because, to put it simply, we do not want the outside world to know exactly what we do. Not that anyone would believe it if we did put into print." He looked at them and gestured around them, saying, "Would any of you have believed all this was here before actually seeing it with your own two eyes?"

"So, what do you do here, besides providing Sanctuary to mermaids, centaurs, and others as such?" Telara asked, ignoring his question. "No more beating around the bush this time. Exactly what does this have to do with us?"

"Sanctuary, when first created, was to provide a safe haven to any magical being, which includes all the mythicals you have encountered along with the ones you have not, and now including yourselves," Lucius said, as if that explained it all. "Not only do we protect the mythical creatures and give them a life, but we also train the descendants of the gods and goddesses who are either born here or come to us from the outside."

"So there are actual people who live here day-to-day?" Cole asked, looking very interested, his eyes lit up with curiosity along with the eyes of their sci-fi fanatic Chad.

Lucius gave him a look that clearly was saying, "Duh." "Yes, most of the residents, mythical and human alike, were born here at Sanctuary."

"So you have a hospital here?" Chance looked around at all the wilderness surrounding them.

"In your time here, you will discover there is more to Sanctuary than what you have seen. Sanctuary is vast and so are its resources that you will learn more about as time goes on."

"If we choose to stay," Telara interjected. "But you still have not explained how this all pertains to us. Why are we so *honored* to be able to see the glories of Sanctuary?"

Lucius nodded in agreement with her, something she hadn't expected. "As I said, we train the descendants on how to use their unique specialties." Lucius grinned at each of them before finishing. "Or, in the case of you seven, your powers."

"O-o-okay," Telara said slowly. "I think we should leave now." She rose and started to walk away.

"Don't you want to hear about your powers, my dear?"

That stopped her. She turned and looked at him. "What powers?"

He motioned back to her spot and, after a slight hesitation, she sat down.

"Now, where was I?"

"You were going to tell us about our powers." Chad rubbed his hands together in anticipation.

Telara shook her head. *Figures he would be all gung-ho about this mythical voodoo.*

"Right. Well, as I said, we train descendants of the gods to use their powers so they can protect themselves and others. Sanctuary has been around since ancient Greece."

"Let me guess, you trained the mighty Hercules?" Telara interjected with sarcasm.

"Are you going to let me explain or keep making your snide comments?" Lucius asked her and waited until she finally murmured an apology. When she didn't say anymore, he continued. "No, the mighty Hercules was not trained here, but we have been training young heroes for a long time. Throughout the years, many heroes have come and gone, but Sanctuary will always remain to train the new ones. To the outside world, we are an institute that teaches 'special' children and, if anyone tries to investigate us, they suddenly get the feeling as if all is right and that we are what we say we are. The mystical power of Sanctuary keeps outsiders from probing into our business. Everyone, including your parents, who I am sure did their best to check into our intents, decides we are what we say we are."

"So we are what? Demigods?" Cole's eyes lit up at this thought. "Static!"

Lucius threw back his head and laughed. "Not quite, my young friend." Lucius seemed to take much amusement in the reactions of the three guys. "Yes, you are descendants, and yes, you do carry the blood of gods in your veins. But a demigod is someone with a godly parent, and to my knowledge, none exist in this day and age."

"May I ask why?" Vanna asked and then apologized for interrupting.

"Do not apologize for innocent curiosity," Lucius said, smiling at her and earning a glare from Telara, who felt the rebuke from his statement. "During the Hellenistic period, the Greek gods seemed to take a hiatus, if you may. They no longer visited the world of man, whether to have dalliances or to let their presence be known." Lucius ignored Cole's and Chad's snickering over him saying dalliances and continued. "They kept to themselves and were not heard from again. As this was very unusual for the gods to do, many believed that they vanished as people's belief in them had. But yes, their children still lived and had children of their own." Lucius gestured toward each of them. "Hence, the seven of you."

"So that would make our parents children of gods then," Chad said. "Why wouldn't they tell us this?"

"Somehow, I don't think it would be a very good dinner conversation," Chance told his brother.

"Actually," Lucius broke in before a fight could break out. "I would say your parents do not even know. Not all children of the gods inherit the bloodline giving them power. It is why I go across the globe seeking out the children where the bloodline has appeared and bring them here to help them with their power and prepare them for what is to come. Are you ready to discover all about yourselves?"

"We haven't decided whether we are staying yet or not," Telara objected.

Lucius inclined his head. "Well, then I will leave you to discuss among yourselves. When you make your decision, I will be over by the equipment shed, just give a yell." He walked over to the shed farthest from them as if giving them privacy.

"Telara, are you nuts?" Chad asked. "You really want to leave before we find out our powers?"

"If we have any powers." Telara leaned down on her elbows. "I mean, are we for sure Tia's gust of wind was not some fluke to make us think she has some sort of magical powers?"

"You are forgetting all the weird stuff that has happened to us over the past few years," Vanna pointed out.

"That doesn't mean we have any type of powers. It just means that weird stuff happens around us," Telara protested.

"This is not the first time Tia has conjured up gusts of wind," I.Q. pointed out.

Telara stared at him with her mouth open. Out of all her friends, I.Q. was the one who she expected to be on her side. He was the scientist who discovered a reason for anything out of the norm.

"Remember when Raven and her cronies were picking on that new girl last year because she was wearing braces? When Tia decked her, that gust of wind knocked not only the posters off the wall but her friends on their butts also."

"There was a door open in the hallway," Telara protested. "You were the one to point that out."

"There was no wind that day Telly," I.Q. shrugged. "I just didn't point it out when I discovered it. I was looking for a reason for it to happen. We also hadn't just spent a week training with a centaur or getting attacked by fairies either."

"Think of all the other mishaps that have happened to us," Vanna said softly. "I mean, the drinking fountain exploding in the school hallway as we passed or sprinklers that suddenly would come on. Electrical appliances that would work just fine until we had something to do with them, Raven was always quick to point it out. That is why she called us the Black Cat Squad and said we were omens for bad luck."

"That has been most of our lives," Cole grumbled.

"Wouldn't it be nice to finally understand all that has happened to us and maybe learn how to control it?" Tia asked her with a half-smile.

"So, you all wanna stay?" Telara asked, feeling as if they were all against her.

"We are not siding against you, Telly," Vanna hastened to assure her. "We would just like to see if there is anything to this. If not, it would definitely be an adventure. I mean, who else can say they have swam with mermaids, trained with a centaur, or even had a trick played on them by a mischievous wood nymph?"

Telara found it hard to argue when Vanna happened to use her own thoughts against her, thoughts Vanna knew nothing about.

"Well, if you guys are in, I might as well stay and keep the boys out of trouble." Telara tried to smile for them.

"Hey!" Cole protested. "You make it sound like I am always in trouble."

Chad nodded in agreement with the same affronted look on his face.

"That's because you are," Tia pointed out to him.

Before this could end up in another Tia vs. Cole war, Telara hollered for Lucius to tell him they had made their decision.

"So, you have decided to stay and see what Sanctuary has to offer," Lucius stated more than questioned.

"You don't have to look so smug about it," Telara grumbled. "But yeah, we are staying."

Chad piped up before Telara could do any more damage. "So, how do we figure out our powers? Tia is the only one who has shown any sign."

"You think so?"

"We know so," Chance said. "None of us have done anything extraordinary since being here."

Lucius gave Telara a searching glance before turning back to Chance. "Brom tells me you almost managed to catch her that evening you went for a swim. She said if not for Raphael, you would have had her by the tail, so to say," Lucius chuckled with a twinkle in his eye. "Her ego was rather dented that a mere mortal, one with god blood aside, of course, came close to her and her hiding spot."

"What can I say...I was always told I am half fish. I am the best swimmer our team has," Chance said in a matter-of-fact way, without any gloating, mainly because he was right and it was well-known.

"Yes, your mastery over the water element would give you one fair advantage."

"You saying I didn't earn my ability?" Chance asked indignantly.

"Of course not," Lucius protested. "None of you knew your powers beforehand, so you could not influence them. Your abilities are your own, but your power has always been there. Did you not wonder how you could have stayed underwater as long as you did while looking for Brom?"

"Never really thought about it," Chance said with a thoughtful expression on his face.

"Okay…Tia has the power of wind, and my dorky brother has the power of water," Chad piped up, ignoring the glare from his brother.

"Correct."

"So, what about the rest of us?"

"That is what I have been trying to figure out."

They turned and saw Raphael standing there, staff in hand.

3

TELARA FELL to her knees and watched as a drop of sweat rolled down the bridge of her nose before it fell onto the dirt path on which she knelt. Ever since they had decided to stay to discover what, *if any* Telara thought, powers they possessed, Raphael had become worse than the drill sergeant they thought him to be. He pushed much harder than before and grew more irritated when none of them, besides Tia and Chance, showed any promise of powers.

"Maybe we don't have any powers!" Telara threw at him after one grueling session showed no more promise than any of the others.

"And maybe you are not trying hard enough!" Raphael had slammed the trunk of the tree with his fist in frustration, disturbing the nymph resting in its branches. She glared down at him and bombarded him with acorns before sticking out her tongue and disappearing. He growled at them then declared training was over while he walked away pulling acorns out of his dark locks that tumbled past his shoulder and down his back.

"Go back to your bunk and rest; we will meet again tomorrow."

The look he threw them before he trotted away made them realize they probably weren't going to enjoy the next day but, then again, it seemed par for the course lately.

Drowsy and exhausted, they wandered back to the bungalow where few words were spoken. Each had their own thoughts running rampant in their minds and all pertained to the past few weeks with Raphael. After dropping his big bombshell, Lucius had informed them Raphael would start their training for real.

"You mean to tell us the abuse we have suffered before wasn't real?" Chad had protested, to which Cole had to add, "Tell that to all my bruises and aches."

While they joked, the others had solemn expressions and apprehension about the coming weeks. Telara was still hung up on Lucius's "Prepare for what is to come" comment but, apparently, she was the only one. Chad and Cole were too fired up about the fact they supposedly had powers to care, but there was yet to be any proof of it.

Tia was getting the hang of her wind power and could now create gusts of wind that would blow papers off the tables but anything more she had issues with. Of course, when Cole pointed out to her that maybe she should concentrate more on her power and less on their dark and brooding teacher, she managed to knock him off the table and into the barrel of drinking water, causing many fits of laughter.

Chance could stay underwater for ten minutes without having to come up for air and, during one exercise where he tried to beat that record, he rushed out of the water so fast for air that he caused a wave to crash against the shore, soaking Vanna who was watching. They had done their best to stifle their laughter, not wanting to upset Vanna because, while she was the most even-tempered of them all, she could have the worst temper. Vanna had looked down at her wet clothes and back to the very apologetic Chance and laughed out loud. The others then let their laughter run free.

Other than Tia and Chance, no one else could figure out their powers, no matter how hard Raphael pushed them.

They entered the bungalow and trudged to the kitchen where there were subs waiting for them on the counter. It seemed that whenever they wanted something to eat it would magically appear, almost as if the house itself knew what they needed before they did. After they ate, they went their separate ways, too tired to meet in the game room.

Telara lay down on her bed and stared at the ceiling where shapes were swirling around rapidly as if mimicking her emotions. She frowned as she watched the lines swerve one way then the other. She watched the swirls, circles, and lines chase each other across the ceiling. She smiled as one circle ran from a line, only to get pulled into one of the swirls and disappear. The line that was chasing the circle stopped and jumped over the swirl going after another circle. Telara watched and realized that what she was seeing was the lines and swirls working together to capture the circles.

That's not fair.

Telara watched one circle being pushed toward a swirl.

Duck, Telara commanded and, to her amazement, the circle ducked. Telara looked over at another circle

Help your friend.

That circle joined with the other circle until they resembled a figure eight. The lines and swirls tried to rush this figure.

Hmmm, Telara thought then commanded the other circles rushing around, *Join with your friends and make a chain.*

Across the ceiling was a line of joined circles.

Now, pen them in.

As she watched the chain of circles, reminding her of the paper chains she made as a child for Christmas, moved and wrapped themselves around the lines and swirls. The lines and swirls fought against the chain to no avail until, finally, they gave up and formed into different shapes.

On the ceiling with the chain of circles penning them in, the lines and squiggles made seven different shapes. In the center of the group was a shape that resembled a closed eye: swirls chasing all around as if blowing wind, jagged lines along the bottom flowing like waves, a small line attached to a small circle-like shape that reminded Telara of something, but she couldn't put her finger on it. Other swirls gathered together to form what looked like clouds. Some lines gathered to make several rectangular shapes all clumped together, and the last shape made even less sense: the swirls looked like vertical waves rather than horizontal. No more lines or squiggles remained after creating this seventh symbol. As if their work was now completed, they all became still, frozen on the ceiling in the forms they took. Telara smiled to herself, feeling a bit better, and closed her eyes as sleep finally took over.

That night Telara's dreams were very erratic. One moment, she was standing in a meadow watching fauns and satyrs playing with the nymphs; the next, she was staring at total darkness that was surrounding her slowly until there was no light to be seen. She held her hand up and couldn't see it. She hollered for her friends only to discover her voice had failed her. She started to panic when a voice came from the darkness.

"Iremisoume ligo pyrotechnima mou." The voice was soothing but, in Telara's present state, all that registered was that the voice was speaking in a language she didn't understand.

"What? What are you saying?" she hollered into the darkness, trying to locate the person who spoke so strangely. Again, the voice repeated itself in the same soothing tone. While the voice was calm, Telara was anything but.

"Who are you? Where are you?"

She jerked to her left and her right but saw nothing but blackness. She closed her eyes, willing herself to calm down, but discovered her imagination was her own worst enemy. Her skin felt all clammy, and she swore she felt something crawling up her arm. She opened her eyes and screamed, slapping her arms to get rid of whatever it was. Due to the darkness still surrounding her, she couldn't see what caused her to freak-out.

The voice chuckled, and then she heard, "Katharisete to myalo sas pyrotechnima."

Telara couldn't understand what he, for she was sure the voice was male, a very irritating one, was trying to say. What she did understand was the amusement in his voice, and that did nothing to calm her already churning emotions.

"Who are you? I can't understand what you are saying. Show yourself!" Telara felt the tears streaming down her cheeks, which caused her to grow even angrier.

The voice gave a very unhappy sigh and said, "Den eiste etoimoi na fainetai."

As quickly as the Shadows appeared, they were gone but so were the nymphs, satyrs, and fauns. Telara stared at the bright light glowing in front of her and saw a shadowed shape walking toward her.

Telara jerked straight up in bed, wiping the sweat and tears from her face. She was glad the others were so far away as she was sure she had screamed in her sleep. She glanced at the clock to realize there were hours before she had to get up. She lay back down but found she couldn't close her eyes, so wary was she of the nightmare returning. She stared at the ceiling to see if her circle friends were playing around to distract her, but they too were sound asleep and weren't moving.

She climbed out of her bed and walked over to the window overlooking the lake and trees. She saw the mermaids playing in the water and wondered if they were keeping Chance up as his room was underground with a window so that you could see right into the lake. She remembered the remarks that his brother had made when Chance chose that room as his on their first night there.

Funny his power is over water, and he chooses the room basically in the lake.

Telara looked up the mountain toward the room at the top where her best friend Tia slept.

Tia chose the room up in the clouds, and she has the power of wind. I have the room with the crazy shapes running across the ceiling; maybe my power is insanity.

With that thought, she plopped herself onto the white chair situated next to the window and leaned against the glass.

A buzzing sounded in her ears. She looked around trying to discover the identity of the mysterious noise but after several minutes of looking over everything in her room and leaning down to listen to any device that could be the cause, she gave up and sat back down in the chair.

Guess no sleep for me tonight. Might as well go down to the kitchen and try to find something to eat before our drill sergeant decides to come for another boot camp session.

That is where her friends found her the next morning, eating toast and staring out at nothing.

"Hey, you okay?"

Telara glanced at Vanna, ever the mother hen, and smiled. "I'm fine; I just didn't sleep very well," she told her with a grimace.

"I slept too well, had a hard time pulling myself out of bed." Vanna made herself some toast and sat next to Telara. "Want to talk about it?"

"Nah, don't want to bore you," Telara said, trying to smile for her friends who were all wearing the same worried look.

"You are not going to bore us," Vanna said. "We are your friends. That's what we're here for."

"Leave her be, Van," Tia said. "You know as well as any of us that when she is ready to talk, she will but not before."

Telara gave her a thankful smile.

"Everyone ready for boot camp?" Cole asked with a mouthful of cereal, earning disgusted looks from the others.

"What?" he asked, spitting cereal out which spattered against Vanna.

"Ewww! Cole, can you be any more disgusting?" Vanna walked over to the sink to wash off her arm.

Telara rubbed her eyes, feeling a headache coming on as the buzzing got louder.

"You okay?" Tia asked her quietly so as not to alert the others.

"Yeah, just getting a bit of a headache." Telara smoothed her fingers over her eyebrows as if trying to rub the pain away.

"Maybe you should go back to bed," Tia told her.

"Yeah, I'm sure that would go over well with Raphael," Telara snorted. "Nah, I will be okay." She attempted to give Tia a reassuring smile, but the buzzing seemed to grow louder causing her to grimace instead.

"If you're sure," Tia said, not looking very convinced at all.

Vanna returned to the table still griping at Cole.

RAPHAEL MET THEM AT THE TRAINING FIELDS WITH THE CRYSTAL ball in hand. They groaned. That was one exercise they hadn't been subjected to since Lucius told them of their powers. They took their seats on the picnic tables, giving the ball very nervous glances.

Raphael held up the ball and announced, "This is a power ball. While held in the hands of regular people, it looks like a regular crystal ball. But…" he said tossing the ball to Tia who grabbed it, causing it to glow. "In the hands of power, it will become more."

They watched the ball as it came alive and levitated above Tia's out-stretched hands. There was a swirling mist moving inside the ball. Tia gasped and pulled her hands away, causing the ball to fall to the ground and lose the glow and mists.

Raphael chuckled. "The ball will not harm you but may bring out your individual powers so for today, you will go to the center and play a game of ball."

"Back to playing catch?" Cole asked, his shoulders sagging with disappointment.

"Yes," Raphael answered and motioned for them to start.

Several hours later, along with several bruises, the only ones who could get the ball to give even the slightest of glows were still Tia and Chance. With Chance, the glow was accompanied by water swirling around inside the ball, but he could not get it to levitate as Tia had. Cole was frustrated and threw the ball to the ground while the others were bent over with their hands on their knees breathing hard.

"This is useless," Telara practically growled, the buzzing in her head getting louder with each passing moment. It was so distracting she hadn't heard Vanna's warning when Tia sent the ball toward her, and it smacked her in the shoulder, knocking her down. When Raphael called a halt to make sure she was alright, Telara brushed him off and grabbed the ball again, trying to get it to do anything, but still nothing.

"You need to try…"

Telara whirled on Raphael. "What do you think we're doing?" she shrieked at him, feeling as if she were losing her mind. The buzzing in her head kept her from concentrating on what she was doing.

Raphael looked at her and said with a restrained voice, "If you would let me finish, I was going to say you need to try to clear your mind. It might help you."

Don't say it Telly, please.

Telara looked back at Tia and snapped, "Who said I was going to say anything?" Her friends looked at her strangely. "What?"

"I didn't say anything, Telly," Tia told her slowly.

Telara didn't know what to say at that point. She was sure she had heard Tia say it loud and clear. As a matter of fact, Tia's voice overrode all the buzzing in her head. She stared at her friends, who were looking at her as if she had lost her mind.

Maybe I have, Telara thought. Instead, she said, "I'm done for the day. I'm going to get something to drink." With that, she turned and strode back to the barracks.

No one spoke until she was a distance away; however, for some reason, she still heard what they said.

"Ummm, Tia, did you say anything?" Vanna asked.

"No," Tia said slowly, watching Telara's retreating back. "But I was thinking it."

Raphael overheard the exchange but made no comment other than to tell them they were done for the day. They were to relax and meet again the following morning. They grumbled but slowly followed Telara back to the barracks.

4

———

RATHER THAN GO to the game room to relax with her friends, Telara went straight to her room and curled up in the chair, staring out the window to find some calm. She wasn't sure how long she was there, but the light was fading, and the sky had a reddish glow when she heard a tentative knock on her door. She didn't even need to ask who it was; there was only one person who would come to her room after such a blow-up.

"Come in," Telara said, feeling a bit sheepish for yelling at her best friend. She looked over as Tia came in with a steaming bowl.

"Tomato soup," Tia announced. "Remember our moms making that for us whenever we were feeling off-kilter?" she asked with a smile.

"Ti-," Telara started to apologize, but Tia held up her hand.

"Don't apologize," she said. "We have all been under lots of stress this past week and one of us was bound to blow up at one point. I'm just glad it wasn't Van." They both chuckled. None of them could handle when Vanna lost her temper which, fortunately, was rare. "Forget it."

"I guess I am just hearing things," Telara said.

"I may not have said it," Tia said hesitantly, causing Telara to look up at her, "But I was thinking it."

Telara shook her head "I guess we have been friends for so long I know what you are going to say before you say it." How many times had they been mistaken for twins in their lives? Their looks were so close except for their eye color. Telara's was a deeper blue than Tia's baby blues. They had the connection of twins, even more so than Telara had with her own twin. Telara was sure that is what it was.

She took the soup and started sipping it, anything to keep her mind preoccupied from her blow up. Tia was watching her closely, and Telara could almost hear the doubt pouring off her at that statement. Tia sat down on the bed, gave her a thoughtful look, and opened her mouth as if to say something. Then, thinking better of it, she pursed her lips together. Tia knew her friend well enough to know that right now Telara's mind was as closed tight as a miser's fist around a shiny new penny, as their parents would say. Now wasn't the time to bring up what she and Van had talked about during their walk back to the bungalow. She decided the best course of action to take would be to change the subject.

"Wanna come down and play some pool?" Tia asked. "Chance said he might even let you win this time." Chance wasn't only a jock when it came to the water, he could play most games with the athletic skill that Telara envied at times.

Telara smiled. "Thanks, but I think right now I just want to be by myself. I need some alone time right now. Maybe later when I feel more like myself."

"Okay, but remember we are all here for you. Don't shut yourself off from us, Telly. We have been through too much together to let anything drive us apart, even a supernatural world with bunches of mythical voodoo."

Telara smiled at her. "You all worry too much."

Telara understood what Tia was trying to say, but she really did need some time to herself. She knew she had a quick fuse when lit, but it never had been directed at her friends. Besides, when she was alone, the buzzing didn't seem quite as bad.

"Maybe," Tia said. "Well, I am going to go before Chad and Chance kill each other over the pool table. It would be hell getting out all the blood."

Telara chuckled but continued to stare out the window, feeling the buzzing in her head rise again in volume. How was she going to tell her friends she was scared she was losing her mind? The buzzing was driving her insane. It had started during their first week, but it had not been enough to bother her until today. Today, it was so loud that she felt as if thousands of bees had taken to swarming around in her head. She looked down at the bowl in surprise as she realized she had finished the soup. She put the bowl down and got ready for bed. She suddenly felt so tired that she could not keep her eyes open. Maybe she could escape the buzzing in sleep.

No nightmares tonight, she prayed as she lay under the covers and stared at the ceiling where the same moving shapes were chasing each other from one end to another. This time, though, she didn't have the energy to try to figure out the pattern. She watched them until their movements lulled her to sleep.

When she opened her eyes, she was standing outside by the lake on the shore. She looked into the lake to see the mermaids splashing about.

Oh no, not again.

She moved away from the lake as if it would stop what was about to happen.

Please not again.

She felt the darkness this time before she could see it swirl around her.

"Go away," she shouted.

But, just as before, the darkness kept coming and wrapping its dark tentacles around her until there was no light. She fell to her knees as tears fell down her cheeks.

"Just go away," she moaned, closing her eyes as tightly as a child hiding from the monster underneath the bed.

Please just go away.

Telara wrapped her arms around her knees and started rocking back and forth, trying to shut out the darkness that wrapped itself around her. Telara shook her head, refusing to open her eyes. She felt as if a hand was lifting her chin up. She opened her eyes and saw nothing but blackness. As she continued to stare into the darkness, she could swear she saw a pair of dark eyes staring at her. It was as if they were part of the darkness trying to pull her forward.

"Katharisete to myalo sas pyrotechnima," the deep voice from before said again.

Telara looked at the dark eyes beckoning her forward, trying to discern if that was where the voice was coming from. She wasn't sure how she knew, but she knew those eyes didn't belong to the deep voice talking to her. The dark eyes seemed to grab ahold of her, and she felt herself rising as if she had no control over her body any longer.

"Tin katapolemisi tis pyrotechnima skotadi," the deep voice said again, pulling Telara out of her stupor and giving her the strength to yank herself away from the hold the dark eyes had upon her. She stumbled back from the eyes but still was in the embrace of the shadowy tendrils that were everywhere.

"Oti ena koritsi. Tora antepitethoun."

"I can't understand you," Telara shouted into the darkness, feeling frustrated. The voice sounded so encouraging that she wanted to do whatever it asked her to do if only she knew what that was.

"Please, tell me what you are saying," she said, almost choking from the fear growing within her.

"Chrisimopoilsei ti dynami sas," the voice answered back, making Telara scream in frustration.

"Dammit! I don't know what you are saying!" she screamed, banging her fists on the darkened ground. She laid her head on the ground, feeling as helpless as a babe and hating the feeling along with the deep voice speaking to her in a language she didn't know.

"To gegonos afto mas odigei pouthena," said the disembodied voice before she felt the presence disappear.

"No, don't go!" she shouted. "Please, don't leave me all alone… help me." The last was said on a whimper as she again closed her eyes, feeling more tears flowing down her cheeks. "I can't do this alone. I don't know what I am supposed to be doing."

Telara opened her eyes. She was once again in her room, and the darkness was nowhere to be found. She took a deep breath and laid her head back on the pillow, feeling a strong sense of relief. If those nightmares didn't cease, she would end up crazy. She fought the urge to seek out Tia and tell her about them, she didn't want to burden her friend with her craziness, nor did she want to hear her friend tell her there was nothing to be scared of. She looked up at the ceiling to see what mischief her little friends had gotten to while she slept, only to discover they were once again trapped in the Christmas ring and the same symbols they had created just the other night.

Wait! Was the eye symbol fully open now?

Telara closed her eyes tightly and reopened them and, sure enough, the eye symbol was staring down at her. The center of the eye was as stormy as her mind right now. Telara felt a shiver run down her spine as the eye continued to stare right through her.

She quickly jerked out of bed and went to sit in her chair by the window, not wanting to look at the eye anymore, hoping if she ignored it, it would go away and the next time she looked up, she would see her friends playing like normal.

Normal, Telara thought. *I am not even sure what that is anymore.*

She thought of her friends who were all peacefully sleeping in their rooms right now… or were they? Did they dream of Shadows and eerie black eyes staring out from them? Did they hear the same voice speaking to them in another language as if wanting to help them? Did they have the same nightmares and were just too scared to speak of them as she was? Too many questions and not enough answers.

Only one way to find out. Telara felt a flash of determination at this thought. *Tomorrow, I will have to talk to them to see if I am the only one with these dreams.*

With that final thought, Telara felt better as she now had a goal; a goal that gave her focus and hopefully, after tomorrow, there would be a solution. I.Q. could figure out any puzzle; hopefully, this would be one of them. Telara looked down at the very still lake in the moonlight. There were no mermaids playing in the lake this time nor was there any movement in the trees.

Everyone else seems to be enjoying a night of blissful sleep. Wish I could join them.

A movement by the door caught her eye, and she jerked around, her heart beating fast in her chest.

5

———

STANDING THERE by the door stood a guy who looked around her age, smiling at her as if he was an old friend just stopping in to say hi. His eyes were a dull green with blue flecks, almost reminding Telara of the lake right outside her window. They also seemed as if they belonged to someone much older than his appearance. He just stood there saying nothing as Telara took in his appearance. His hair was a dark brown, almost black, with some very dark streaks that stood out. He was wearing a pair of jeans with a plain black short sleeve shirt. On his feet was a pair of sneakers that were also black.

Man, this guy has the bad boy attire down, Telara thought, liking what she saw. Her gaze came back to his face to see his smile widen a bit but yet it still could not brighten up the dullness of his eyes. She wondered if he could hear her thoughts. He seemed so familiar to her; yet, she could not place where she had seen him before.

Then she realized that he was standing in her bedroom without an invitation and felt instantly on the defense.

"Who are you?" she asked him but, to her amazement, he

just stared at her with that infernal smile. "Can you speak?" she asked him, starting to wonder if he was as crazy as she felt.

"Ela mazi mou."

Telara felt as if the world itself tilted, and she was instantly off balance. That voice! She knew that voice. It had the same deep baritone with the slight accent from her dreams, in a language she didn't understand but with the same soothing affect. Telara shook her head

"I still can't understand what you're saying." she said and saw him hold out his hand to her and motioned for her to take it.

"I think I should get back to bed," she said, slowly moving to the bed only to stop and feel as if she had been sucker punched in the gut. There laying on her bed sound asleep was….her.

"I think I am going to be sick," she said, holding her stomach, still staring at her sleeping figure. She looked over at the guy standing by the door

"Am I…..dead?" she asked haltingly, not sure if she wanted the answer or not. He tilted his head as if he could not understand what she was saying.

Which would fit since I don't understand a word that is coming from his mouth.

She leaned down on the bed to see if she was still breathing and gave a huge sigh of relief when she realized that she was, in fact, still breathing. She turned back to the guy who again held out his hand and repeated himself, this time slowly.

"Guess I don't have much choice at this point," she said in a resigned voice and motioned for him to lead and she would follow.

He gave her another of his smiles and started out the door with her close behind him. She gave her sleeping figure one final glance before walking out of the room and down the hall, heading wherever the stranger was taking her.

And here I was brought up to never go anywhere with a stranger. Although I don't think that mom and dad ever thought I would have an out of body experience like this. Telara gave a deep sigh and just shook her head when the guy gave her a curious look.

"So, ummmm, what do I call you?" she asked and when he gave her a weird look, she went on to explain, "Your name."

When she got no answer, she pointed to herself and said, "Telara." Then she pointed to him with a shrug. "You?"

She got no answer and had to hurry up before he left her behind. "Okay," she muttered. "I guess I can call you Bright Eyes then." She chuckled at that because that would be the last description anyone would give him but for some reason she felt it suited him. "Okay, Bright Eyes, where are we going?"

He didn't answer. He just kept walking down the hall through the common room where, to her surprise, sat Lucius and some older lanky looking man at the table. Where Lucius had a masculine physique, this guy looked like he could be related to Pee Wee Herman. Telara stopped in her tracks and shook her head when Bright Eyes motioned for her to keep following. He gave her a quizzical stare and held out his hand again.

"Erchontai."

She shook her head again and looked over towards where Lucius and the new man were sitting in deep discussion. He looked over at them and then smiled and shook his head as if to say not to worry. He held out his hand again, but she backed away from him, not wanting to draw Lucius's or the stranger's attention to her. Her hand brushed one of the many crystal sconces along the wall and while it didn't move the crystal; it actually went right through her hand as if she was a ghost. The crystal glowed brightly then hummed. Telara was shocked as she had watched her hand go right through the crystal and, feeling very much freaked out, she jerked her hand away from the crystal and watched as the crystal went silent.

Telara held her hand to her chest and looked back at the two men who had suddenly stopped talking and were now starring directly at her, causing her to hold her breath. She waited for Lucius to demand why she was out of bed.

To her amazement, after one cursory glance at the now silent crystal, the stranger turned to Lucius and asked, "So their powers are starting to show?"

"It would appear so," Lucius, still staring right at Telara, answered him. Then he smiled, turned back to the stranger, and resumed their conversation as if Telara was not still standing there. "Have the preparations been made?"

"I hope you know what you are doing," the stranger said, running his hands through his hair in an agitated manner. "Going against protocol has never worked in the past. Remember that, Lucius."

Since Lucius was no longer staring at her, she took the time to notice that while at first glance she would call the stranger old, upon more inspection she realized that he was not that old. While there was more grey throughout his hair, some black peered through. His face didn't seem to have as many wrinkles although there were still what her mother would call stress lines, and his eyes definitely had the look of someone who had seen much. She still thought he looked like Pee Wee Herman. Around his neck, she noticed a crystal shard hanging from a chain. She looked back at the crystal sconce on the wall.

Man, this place sure has a thing for crystals.

"I am open to any suggestions that you may have," Lucius told him.

The stranger just leaned back in his chair as if trying to put what was in his mind into words. Again, Bright Eyes grabbed Telara's hand and pulled her forward.

"Erchontai."

Telara grudgingly followed but pulled back a bit trying to hear what they were talking about. But while Telara was interested to hear what they had to say, Bright Eyes did not seem to think it of much importance, so Telara found herself being pulled along down the stairway and past not only the doorway leading down to Cole's room but also right past Chad's.

They stopped right outside of Chance's room, and Bright Eyes pushed open the door and motioned for her to enter. Telara paused right outside, suddenly feeling like an intruder. Sure back home she had been in Chance's room many of times, although not usually by herself and not with some stranger she met in her dreams. But this – this felt wrong somehow. Bright Eyes, oblivious to her plight, pulled her into the room. She walked in and looked around the room towards the window that covered over half the room. There on the other side was the lake and its inhabitants frolicking to and fro. She saw Brom swimming up to the glass and staring down at the sleeping Chance like a love sick teenager. She realized that Brom paid her and Bright Eyes about as much attention as Lucius and the stranger.

So no one can see us. That is good, I guess.

She looked over at Bright Eyes who was also watching the mermaid staring at Chance with somewhat of a wistful look to his face. Telara could almost feel the melancholy rolling off of him, even if she did not understand the cause. It filled the room, causing her to fidget in discomfort.

"Okay, you got me here. Now what?" Telara asked him, pulling him out of his reverie.

He looked at her then back down to Chance and said, "Exaerosis nerou."

Telara groaned.

Not again.

"Look, I don't know what you are saying," she told him, getting very exasperated.

Instead of getting flustered himself, he pointed to Chance then to the window and repeated himself. She looked over at Bromhilda, and he shook his head.

"Ochi. Exaerosis nerou." He pointed to the glass and made a wavy motion with his hand. Telara looked back and forth then understood.

"Water," she said, and he smiled and nodded his head as if to say finally.

"Okay, water," she said. "What about it?"

He again pointed to Chance and said, "Exaerosis nerou." Then he pointed to the water outside the window. Telara looked again and then began to realize what he was saying.

"Chance's powers are water."

He nodded to her with a smile then motioned for her to follow him yet again.

Here we go.

But follow him she did.

This time, he took her through a doorway that they had never seen before. Telara noticed that there were stairs that went up into the mountain and also ones that also went down. Bright Eyes motioned for her to follow him up the stairs, and they entered Tia's room. There, they saw her friend deep asleep on her bed that seemed as if it was floating in midair. Telara was sure that the bed had not done that before.

"Aioliki peripatitis," he said, pointing at Tia and her floating bed. And if it was not for what had happened with Chance, she would have been lost but this time, she felt for sure she knew what he was saying.

"The power of the wind," she said, and he nodded with a smile.

"Yes, we already know that Chance has water power and Tia has wind power," she said, feeling very much aggravated at all this madness. "If all you are going to do is drag me around and tell me stuff that I already know than I am going back to bed." Telara had only taken five steps when she stopped and turned back around to face him.

"Ummmm….how do I go back to bed?" she asked, feeling very uncertain as what to do with her sleeping body back in her bed. She did not want to get back down there and stare at herself for the rest of the night.

He jerked his head, motioning for her to follow him yet again.

"Like I have much of a choice," she grumbled and followed him to I.Q.'s room that was not far from Tia's.

Just like in Chance's room and then Tia's, he pointed at the sleeping teenager and this time said, "Astrapi epithetikos." Then, he pointed up, causing Telara to look up. She could see storm clouds brewing where the ceiling should have been.

"He has the power over the weather?" Telara asked to which he shook his head and pointed up yet again. "I am sorry, but I don't understand what you are trying to say," she told him.

He grabbed her hand, leading her over to a static ball that

sat on the table. He put her hand on it, and she felt the electricity give her a tiny shock.

"Electricity?" she asked to which he gave her a quizzical look.

He glanced around the room as if looking for something specific. He gave her a very frustrated look as if to say it was all her fault that he could not find what he was looking for. Then, he turned his head quickly as if he had heard a sound. Telara looked around but could not hear anything other than their breathing and heart beats. Then, he grabbed her hand and pulled at her yet again.

She followed him to the staircase outside of I.Q.'s room and down two flights until they came out in the basement where they had visited Chance's room. Then, he pulled her through the doorway and down a set of stairs leading to Cole's room. It was as warm as a sauna. Cole has always been one who liked the heat, so this did not surprise Telara much. She looked around the room and realized that the walls reminded her of moving molten lava that you would see in a movie. She never realized that before. She went to touch the walls and while they were warm to the touch, they did not burn her hand. She looked back at Bright Eyes.

He smiled and then pointed to Cole saying, "Fotia miza."

She looked at Cole and some things started to fall into place, like the time that he was blamed for starting a fire in grade school after throwing a rolled up ball of paper into the trash bin when he was angry for getting a bad grade on a test that he actually tried on. Or the time that he set off the water sprinklers in the lunchroom after arguing with a jock over a girl they both had dated.

She looked at Bright Eyes and simply said, "Fire."

He smiled and nodded. Then, they were off again back up the stairs to Chad's room that was next to Cole's room.

There, Chad was sleeping soundly, and Telara felt a chill in the air. Suddenly, she knew just as she knew with Cole.

"Pago michani," Bright Eyes told her.

She said in a very matter of fact tone of voice, "Ice." To which he again smiled and nodded.

They went past Chance's room and down the hallway that they had always believed was a dead end. *Well, until tonight,* Telara amended. Bright Eyes smiled at her as if he could read her thoughts. There was a wooden wall that Bright Eyes touched, causing it to open, and Telara saw the stairs they had used earlier. They followed it up into the hallway leading to Vanna's room. Up the winding staircase they went until they were standing in her room. Vanna's room was built right into the great tree that loomed over the place they had come to call home recently.

He pointed to her and said, "I mitera fysi."

Telara looked around the room, seeing all the plants and the walls that were, in fact, the inside of the tree. She looked at Bright Eyes saying hesitantly, "Power over plants?"

He cocked his head as if in thought and gave a hesitant nod as if to say partially. She looked back over at Vanna and her bed made out of wood and the flowers that surrounded the bed.

"Our little mother nature," she murmured to herself and saw him smile with approval.

Finally, they ended back at her room with her staring down at her sleeping form, feeling a bit creeped out.

She turned to him and asked, "So is this my power?" She motioned to herself and her sleeping form. He smiled a sad smile, and she was not so sure she liked that smile as much as she did the others.

He pointed to her and said, "Myalo Klinon." He did not seem very happy about that and gave her a look of sympathy before slowly disappearing right before her eyes.

"Hey," she yelled. "Don't leave. You haven't told me my power."

But it was too late as he was gone, and she was again alone in her room staring down at her sleeping body.

Okay-y-y-y, now what?

She thought about hollering for Bright Eyes to come back and tell her how to get back into her body but with their language barrier, it probably wouldn't get her anywhere. She flopped down on her bed with a sigh, and then realized that during this whole time with Bright Eyes there was no buzzing in her head. She smiled at that thought, finally feeling more like herself - even with the weirdness of this place. She closed her eyes and felt herself relax.

6

———

THE NEXT MORNING, all the shapes on the ceiling had gone back to their erratic designs that was the norm for daytime. At least, there was no eyeball staring down at her now. At breakfast, she told her friends about her nighttime wanderings, leaving nothing out. Her friends were skeptical at first, which was to be expected considering she was skeptical during her experience, but after Telara told them about Tia's floating bed and I. Q.'s stormy ceiling, they were convinced. Tia and I.Q. verified that information as both had come to that discovery in the past week. The only reason they had not told anyone was because they were unsure if they were losing their minds.

"Well, I would say you were definitely in our rooms last night," Chance said. "But didn't you say you saw your own body and stood right in front of Lucius and whoever without them seeing you? How is that even possible?"

"That is exactly what I am saying! I don't know how it is possible, but it happened," Telara told them. Vanna seemed to be watching her very intently. "What?" Telara asked her waiting for Van to tell her that she was losing her mind.

"Nothing really, but you don't seem so stressed out anymore. The bags are gone from under your eyes; yet, it seemed you still did not get any sleep," Vanna told her, still staring right at her.

Telara shifted a bit, feeling very uncomfortable. What with her nighttime trip around the bungalow, she had completely forgotten about her decision to tell them of the nightmares and was feeling a bit apprehensive about doing so now. But they were her best friends, and they were in the same boat as she and deserved to hear the truth. Therefore, she told them about how since they had arrived here she had started getting nightmares and how with each day they had seemed to intensify, until the culmination of last night.

"So that would explain your curtness lately," Vanna said with a sympathetic look.

"Sorry guys," Telara said, feeling like a heel for not trusting her friends enough to tell them all about everything before.

"Did you really think we would think you were nuts just because of a few nightmares?" Tia asked her, making her feel even worse.

"Yeah, we know you are crazy without the nightmares," Chad joked, earning him an elbow in the ribs from Vanna. "Hey, come on! She hangs out with us; you have to be crazy to do that." That one got a few chuckles and even Telara smiled.

"There it is," Cole said excitedly, pointing right at Telara. She looked around trying to find what it was that Cole was so excited about.

"Where what is?" she asked confused.

"The smile that we have all been missing," he told her, pulling another smile from her.

She opened her mouth to apologize, but Tia interrupted her. "No more apologies. That is what friends are all about, being a butthead and not having to apologize for it." Telara had to agree there; she knew if the situation was reversed, she would not expect it from any of them, so she just smiled at her friends and sent up thanks for the friends that sat with her at that table.

"Okay so now that the mushiness is over, let's talk about this dream guy of yours," Tia said with a gleam in her eyes. "Was he cute?"

The guys groaned over this, but Telara just smiled.

"Yup" was her only answer and before Tia could ask anymore, Chad interrupted her.

"Forget the guy! Let's talk about the powers. You said I have the power over ice?"

Telara laughed and repeated the experience; one could not call it a dream if it had actually happened could they? I.Q. seemed really interested in the language that Bright Eyes was speaking and had her try to repeat some. Telara, not knowing the language, did her best, but she was sure she got it wrong, and I.Q. agreed with her.

"So, he called you a Klingon?" Cole laughed. Telara just glared at him along with Tia who reached out and smacked him.

"That is what it sounded like," Telara said defensively.

"What about what he called Cole?" I.Q. asked again.

"Fotia Meza," she said slowly.

"Fotia is fire in Greek, so my guess would be that your visitor is most likely Greek," I.Q. declared, his brows knitted together in thought.

"Greeks don't speak English?" Chance asked.

"I am sure there are some that might still stick to the old ways, but then again, this might not even be a person who is alive," I.Q. said thoughtfully, giving Telara chills with the thought that there might be some ghost visiting her at night causing her to have some out of body experiences.

"Great! We get to stay in a place that is haunted." Chad's eyes lit up as if that thought excited him, his hazel eyes turning almost green in his excitement. He turned to I.Q. "So how do we figure out who the ghost is?"

I.Q. gave him a look that screamed, "Really?" The others laughed, and it was Vanna who answered for him.

"Just because I.Q. is the smartest guy we know doesn't mean he knows how to converse with ghosts." I.Q.'s face turned a shade of pink at the compliment.

"But I.Q. knows everything," Chad told her to which I.Q. just snorted.

"Just because I know how to open my school books and study does not mean I know everything. It just means that I care more about my education rather than which girl is on the rebound and easy prey or what NASCAR racer made the poll this race."

"Oh yeah! Speaking of which…" Chad said, only to get interrupted by I.Q.

"I was not speaking of which," he said and before Chad could say anything, he went on to say, "But I would say this guy is definitely Greek - whether alive or no we don't know. There is only one of us who could probably even get that information." He glanced at Telara, but she just shivered. It seemed the only contact she had with the guy in question had to do with her nightmares, and she really did not want to have to go through that again to get some information. Of course, that was never in her control anyways. "But that is neither here nor there right now. I would say that he has helped us enough to figure out our powers."

"Yeah, all but yours and Telara's," Cole said, and they nodded their heads in agreement.

"True, but there is always a way to find that out," Chance said with a smile. They looked at him and waited for him to continue. "Raphael sent one of the little guys to tell us to take a break today." He started smiling regarding his own nickname for those satyrs, one that irritated them to no end. "He is meeting with Lucius and some other people for a meeting, so we have the day to ourselves and a training field at our disposal." They groaned at that, considering how their training had gone and how frustrating it was for them. "There is also that power ball there that Tia and I managed to use. I mean, without someone there barking at us maybe we could manage it. No pressure."

Now that idea had some merit in Telara's mind. After all, without someone telling her to keep concentrating with all the buzzing, which right now seemed to be very minimal, maybe she could try.

"It's worth a try." She shrugged, not really looking forward to it.

"Yeah, but this time let's just play and see what happens," Tia suggested. When they asked what she meant, she told them, "Let's play a game of volleyball." At the protests that the ball was too heavy to do that, she shook her head. "It felt light to me. Maybe if I am the one who serves it, maybe it will do the same with you guys."

"Or we could end up with some heavy-duty bruises," Cole grumbled.

"I say let's try it," Telara said, and they agreed.

After breakfast, they strolled down to the fields, watching to make sure there were no others there to watch their attempts. If they failed, they really did not want to become any more of entertainment than they already were. While they never said anything, they could still hear the giggles and chuckles from the wood nymphs and others that inhabited the forest around them whenever they messed up one of their trainings. Luckily for them, when they reached the field, there was not even a woodland animal about. This really made Telara feel good and start to feel a bit positive about this.

Chance found the power ball and held it in his hand. As they watched, it seemed to fill with water. Then he smiled and seemed to push the ball off his hand with a jet of water, sending it sailing to Tia. Without thinking, she caught it without it touching her hands. They could see the ball drain of water and the mists start swirling around inside. She grinned and sent it sailing towards Telara, who caught it with her hands. The mist disappeared, but nothing else happened. Telara grimaced but after some encouragement from her friends, she tossed it to Chad. He held out his hands and caught the ball but still nothing. He shrugged and tossed it to Cole with the same outcome. They had all agreed not to get frustrated, so he just smiled and threw it in the air and caught it before sending it to Tia who again caught it with the mist. This went on for several more minutes, and they lost track of time.

They paired off with I.Q., Vanna, Chance, and Cole to one side while Telara, Tia, and Chad were teamed up on the other side. They tossed the ball back and forth to each other over their invisible net in between. Telara was starting to really get into the game. She could feel all the tension leaving her body, and the buzzing in her head was completely gone. Volleyball was something they all enjoyed doing, and she was starting to feel at home even if it didn't really constitute as an actual game. Once, Tia put too much oomph in her flick of the wrist, and the ball sailed over Cole's head, earning her a nice little glare.

"That would be a point to us," she told him, grinning even broader when he gave her a look of promised retribution.

He grabbed the ball, tossed it in, and prepared to serve it right past them. Telara held her breath, hoping he would not hurt his hand as this was not a regular ball. However, when his hand connected with the ball, it seemed to come alive. Flames flickered inside the ball, and it sailed right towards them. Telara watched the ball knowing that at that rate, they would not be able to stop it. Tia was not about to let Cole outdo her. She concentrated on the ball and as it went to soar over her head, she jumped up and managed to connect with the ball, sending it back towards Cole, who was standing there with his mouth wide open.

This turn of events seemed to cause them all to pause; all except Tia, who was smiling at Cole as the ball flew past his left ear and landed carelessly on the ground behind him.

"What?" she asked them, not understanding why they were staring at her.

"You just jumped over three feet in the air," Telara told her, staring at her in awe. "Looks like this game just got more interesting."

"I did not. I just jumped for the ball," she told them then looked at the others to see that they were shaking their heads. "Really?" she asked.

"Yeah, Cole's firepower sent it flying waaayyy over our heads," Chad said with a smile, starting to come down from his momentary shock. "But you saved the day." He chuckled, shaking his head. He looked back at the others. "Well, that is two to us. Your serve," he said still smiling. "Come on guys! Let's play!"

They let out with their whooping and hollering, feeling as if there was no pressure; just friends who were playing a regular game of volleyball - well, with a twist.

This time, Chance grabbed the ball and, with a very wet splash, sent it towards his brother who caught the ball. This time, they watched as the water froze, and there was a misting of ice over the ball. Chad didn't stop to wonder at this. He just lifted the now very light ball and sent it towards Vanna. She attempted to set it up for Chance to send but instead, as it lifted from her fingers, they watched as a root from the ground popped up and sent it back towards the others. Telara laughed at that and lunged for the ball. The ball went back to being crystal, but she didn't let that bother her. They were there to have fun, and she was having as much fun just watching her friends show off their power. Telara felt freer than she had since coming to this place, and she was not about to let a little thing like a crystal ball bring her down now.

I.Q. shot the ball back to them, and they watched as electricity seemed to spike from the ball. Tia snagged it. She sent it towards Chance, who sent it up in the air with a burst of water that turned into a steam cannon as Cole sent it back towards them. The combination of both seemed to send the ball with such force towards Chad that Tia felt a cold chill creep down her spine. In that split second, she knew without a doubt that it was going too fast for Chad to concentrate enough of his power to stop it without hurting himself. She lunged towards the ball to stop it and, to everyone's amazement, it stopped in mid-air and hung there. The ball then glowed and hovered before gliding over to Telara. Telara just stared at the ball then backed away from it, causing it to drop to the ground with a thud. She looked at the others with a stunned look.

They were startled out of their stunned reverie by the

sound of clapping. They turned around and there in the trees stood not only their drill sergeant Raphael but also Lucius who seemed to have a pleased look on his face. Raphael was staring at Telara with a very concentrated look that had her feeling a bit uneasy.

7

———

THE FEELING of accomplishment from their volleyball game lasted through to the following morning. Tia, mistress of the wind; Chance, Lord of the water; Vanna, their own little mother nature; Chad, sultan of ice; Cole, master over fire; I.Q., keeper of lightning and electricity; and now Telara, the madam of her own mind. The consensus was that Telara's power was what was causing the buzzing in her head. I.Q. seemed to think it was her power trying to assert itself. As her power seemed to levitate the ball, I.Q. said that was a form of telekinesis which is a power of the mind. Telara did not give one fig for the reason; she just prayed now that it had finally shown itself it would keep the buzzing at bay.

Chad spent the morning trying to figure out what God or Goddess they could be related to.

"Chance, Vanna, and I.Q. are easy," he informed them over breakfast. When they just continued to stare at him rather than ask him the questions he wanted them to, he went on to say, "Chance with water has to be related to Poseidon, although with us being related I am not sure how that pertains to me."

He looked thoughtful over that situation for just a moment then continued as if that was not as important right now.

"Vanna, our mother nature, would be related to the Greek of mother nature, Demeter. I.Q., keeper of electricity or lightning as they are the same, has to be related to Zeus, lord of the sky and the great lightning bolt." He leaned back in his chair and smiled as if he had just solved the mystery of life itself.

"And the rest of us, oh mighty one?" Cole asked, fighting the urge to kick out the remaining legs of the chair that were still on the ground. Chance, however, had no reservations, and they laughed as Chad pulled himself off the ground, staring at his brother with a promise of retribution in his glare.

"That will take a bit more thought."

"Let me help you with that."

They looked at I.Q. who had looked very thoughtful while listening to Chad.

"There are more than just the major Gods or Goddesses in Greek mythology such as Eros, Eris, or even Hebe."

"Okay, Eros we all know is cupid; Eris I believe is the Goddess of discord, but Hebe?" Chance asked with genuine curiosity. They had a thing for Greek Mythology and were pretty good with the major ones and some minor, but I.Q., Chad, and even Vanna were more knowledgeable than the rest.

"That is the Goddess of youth," Vanna told him.

"Okay, but what do those have to do with us? I mean, none of us has the power to make someone fall in love – at least, I hope not," Cole said with a shiver, giving Tia a nervous look. It was well-known that Tia did not approve of his Romeo attitude and had repeatedly told him she hoped to be there to see his downfall.

"They were just examples, Cole," I.Q. said, giving him a

frustrated glare. "Now, if you will let me finish without the interruptions…" I.Q. looked around the room and when he was satisfied that they were going to listen, he continued. "Anyways, Aeolus is the God of wind and could possibly be where Tia got her power. There is no God of ice, but there is a God of winter, Boreas."

"Hey! Like the Aurora Borealis," Cole piped up.

"Actually, that is how it got the name: Aurora for the Goddess of dawn and Boreas for the God of winter," I.Q. told him, looking rather impressed that Cole actually put the two together. Usually, unless it had to do with girls or sports, Cole wasn't able to retain much knowledge. Cole gave a smug smile that they ignored.

"Hephaestus was the God of fire and metalworking and also one of the twelve Olympians."

"Ugh!" Cole grimaced. "You mean I am related to the ugly God? Why couldn't it be someone like Adonis?"

"He was also an inventive genius," I.Q. told him, rolling his eyes. "He created many inventions, including the golden chair that was used to imprison Hera. He is considered to be the male counterpart to Athena."

"But he was still deformed," Cole said, wrinkling his nose. He was not about to let that go.

"Okay so now my turn," Telara interrupted so as not to let this friendly discussion turn into an all-out war. I.Q. turned to her giving her a thoughtful look making Telara feel a bit nervous.

"Yes, power of the mind or telekinesis as it is called. That is not an easy one. Athena had the power of wisdom which could be considered the power of the mind in a way, but nothing like what you seem to be able to do. You levitated the power ball causing it to glow."

"Mylo Klingon," Telara murmured. As they gave her funny looks, she went on to explain. "That is what Bright Eyes called me. I wish I knew what it meant." She glared at Cole before he could make another Klingon comment.

They were still deep in discussion when Lucius came and announced that it was time to further their training. They felt uneasy at this announcement, and it was with great trepidation that they followed Lucius. Lucius took them past Mermaid Lake where Brom and her sisters waved at them and invited them to join them for some wet fun. Lucius shook his head and kept walking forward, so he did not notice Brom sticking out her tongue at him. All three sisters gave a pout before disappearing below the water. Flash came over and perched herself on I.Q.'s shoulder as they walked through Fairy Fields. I.Q. did not say anything but kept glancing at her out of the corner of his eyes. Apparently, she had gotten over her annoyance with him as she sat very quietly, for once, while they walked the small path. They expected her to fly away at the border, but she stayed perched on I.Q.'s shoulder.

They walked alongside the mountain that seemed to go on forever; it still amazed them that this place was so well hidden from mortal eyes. Along the way, they tried to get Lucius to tell them which God or Goddess they were apparently related to, but that subject seemed to have him very closed-mouthed.

To their left, Vanna noticed that the woods went from luscious green trees to a sparsely looking thicket of brittle looking trees. There were no colorful flowers along the ground, and trees were smaller in stature. Some even resembled hunched over old people. Gone was the very well-kept forest to be replaced with weeds that seemed to be creeping up the trees, reminding them of a perfect setting for a horror flick.

When Vanna made mention of that to Lucius, they heard a very un-ladylike grunt from Flash. Lucius just chuckled.

"That is the Sprites Domain; they are distant cousins to our friend Flash." Flash glared at that last remark. "No need to be so affronted, little friend. Everyone has relatives that they are not so fond of. But you all should realize that just because they are different from you does not make them more or less of a relative."

Flash gave a harrumph and flew away without a goodbye. Lucius gave a deep sigh. "Fairies and sprites, while very much related, still cannot seem to overcome their differences."

"What differences?" I.Q. asked, watching Flash disappear into the fields.

"Sprites are very mischievous creatures," Lucius began.

Cole laughed at that. "Ummmm... If I remember correctly, Flash has a bit of that herself."

Lucius agreed with him. "Yes, but I wouldn't point that out to her. The fairies are very well-kept in their homes and in their appearances as well. The sprites are more interested in having fun," Lucius explained. "The fairies look down on the sprites for that fact, and the sprites believe the fairies are too 'uppity' I believe is how they put it."

"Ahhhh." Chad seemed to understand. "Kinda like a city slicker going to visit a red neck cousin."

Lucius nodded to that comparison and then pointed to a cave entrance high up the mountain range to their right. "What you see there is Crystal Cave. That is where all the crystals you see around Sanctuary are mined from. The Gnomes of Sanctuary take care of the mining and transportation of the crystals to the Command Center."

"Command Center?" I.Q. asked.

Lucius smiled. "You will see shortly."

Vanna gave a gasp and pointed to what looked like a field that was made out of glass. There were sparkles everywhere the sun touched. There looked to be plants of many colors that were sticking out from the shiny surface. There was also a low stone wall along the way with crystal balls on top all around the wall about five feet apart. They resembled the colorful balls you see in fancy gardens back home.

Vanna took off to investigate close up. Lucius yelled at her to stop, but she had already reached the wall. As she placed her hands on the wall to lean over, they saw the crystals light up. Before they could shout their warnings, Vanna was already sitting on the ground a few feet back from the wall with a dazed look on her face.

"What was that?" Telara demanded of Lucius as they reached Vanna and he was helping her up.

Lucius ignored Telara and was looking Vanna over to make sure she was all right. Then he smiled at her. "I tried to warn you! The field of crystals is the pathway the Gnomes use to transport the crystals to the Command Center. The dust you see all around comes from the crystals they mine. The Gnomes are very protective of the work they do and will tolerate no interference from anyone. What you have just encountered was their security system and a very effective one at that."

Vanna looked at the wall then back at Lucius. "Yeah. Very effective. I don't plan on going near there again." Everyone chuckled at that except for Telara who just glared at Lucius before turning away.

They walked past a grassy hill on their left before they came to another cave in the mountain. This one was on the ground and lit up by crystals along the walls that gave the cave an eerie feeling.

More crystals.

They followed Lucius until they reached the back of the cave and a dead end. On the back wall was a green crystal that glowed as well. Lucius reached up to grasp the crystal, and they watched as the wall gave way and opened for them.

They had to shield their eyes from the brightness that flooded the tunnel. As their vision cleared, their jaws dropped at the sight that greeted them. If Sanctuary was a fairy tale than the room before them was right out of a sci-fi movie set. The cave had opened up to a huge expanse of a room. It looked to have several floors that wrapped around the center courtyard they had just stepped into. In the center of the room was a water fountain made out of white marble. Perched in the center of the fountain was a dragon, approximately the size of an elephant, with its wings widespread as if ready to take flight. It had water spraying from its mouth. The walls all around them were as white as the furniture in their common room. Even the glass in the windows and doors were frosted white so that there was no way to see into the rooms. The only splashes of colors were from the many crystal sconces that lined the walls by each doorway. The few people that they could see wore white lab coats.

What is it with these people and white? Telara wondered.

Lucius motioned for them to follow him through a set of double doors just past the dragon. This room reminded them of a control room that you would see at NASA or someplace similar. On the far wall was a huge screen that was flashing images of different places from around the United States. There were many rows of long desks with computer terminals along the room with a person seated at each; however, rather than the white lab coats, they seemed to be in regular civilian clothing.

This place just keeps getting stranger and stranger, Telara thought.

They followed Lucius to the top row where a guy stood talking with a raven-haired girl, his back towards them.

"May I introduce Ira, the head of the Command Center," Lucius said motioning towards the man who turned and smiled at them. Telara stopped and stared, causing the man to raise his eyebrows at her.

There stood the stranger who Lucius was talking to the night of her dream walk. She didn't want to say anything in front of Lucius; instead, she gave a tight smile and held out her hand.

"Telara," she introduced herself.

"Yes, I know," the man said, and Telara noticed that he was still wearing the crystal necklace around his neck. "And there is Tia, Savanna, Maximillian…"

I.Q. interrupted to say, "You can call me I.Q. or if you want, Max, but please don't use my full name." The others tried to hide their grins; I.Q. has always hated his name and had even been known to put I.Q. on his homework, which would cause many problems though there were several teachers who would let their star pupil get away with most anything.

The man nodded towards I.Q. "Very well, Max," the man stressed, nodding towards I.Q. who nodded back. "Cole, Chad, and Chance," the man finished. "I know all about you and your training under Lucius and your new-found powers that have finally managed to shine through. Let me introduce you to the head of the Alpha faction here at the Command Center."

He motioned to the Raven-haired girl who was standing off to the side with her arms crossed over her chest. Her dark long hair was pulled up into a rather tight ponytail. Rather than a white coat or jeans with a T-shirt, she wore a black shiny looking suit. The suit seemed to stretch with her movements and basically looked to be a second skin rather than an actual outfit. It had long sleeves with pants that had a silver looking belt around the waist. *Very stylish.* Telara wondered if they would be wearing any such outfits but didn't voice it. The girl gave no smile to them, just nodded towards them with a stare that was far from welcoming. Her look was neither friendly nor was it aggressive, but they all had the same feeling that this person didn't care for them.

"Pam will be the one to help you with your crystal training. She is the best here and will be able to better prepare you."

Prepare them? That was the second time they had heard that. Telara turned to Lucius, determined that he was going to answer her this time. But Lucius held up his hand.

"I should have explained before, but our time here grows short; your summer vacation is not nearly long enough. Your powers took longer than anticipated to show and without them, we couldn't have taken this step. I have told you that we're not only here to help you understand your powers but also to help you to be able to use them. Crystal training is a big part of that. I know I'm asking a lot of you, but I'm asking you to trust me. Listen to Pam and let her teach you how to use the crystals. As soon as you're ready, I will tell you all that you need to know. Until then, I ask for your trust."

Telara wanted to argue with him, but they had already decided to stay so, as the saying goes, "in for a penny." Lucius smiled at her waiting for her answer. She gave a small nod of acceptance as she did not trust her voice at this time.

They smiled at Pam and greeted her, but Pam's look didn't change nor did her attitude. She just nodded towards Lucius and Ira and then turned to them.

"If you will follow me, we will get started."

With that said, she started towards the back wall and another crystal that, when she grasped it, another doorway appeared.

They took a deep breath then looked at Lucius who told them, "I will be back after lunch to take you to Raphael." And with that, Ira and he departed, leaving them alone in the room with no choice but to follow Pam out a side door and down the corridor.

This time, when they reached the end of the corridor, the door was already open, and they walked into a room that resembled a school gym. There were tables along one wall with some chairs scattered here and there. There were mats along another side with some racks that seemed to hold staffs of sorts. There were other racks that seemed to hold other types of weapons such as nunchuck-looking things.

"Okay, let me introduce you to the Alpha Faction."

Pam motioned towards the guys and girls that were wearing the same type of suit as Pam's except for some minor differences: short sleeves on one of the guys, one of the girl's neckline was more of a V than the others, but they all wore the same black shimmering material.

"Gage, Sapphire, Trent, Donny, and Stella."

Each person nodded as their name was called out, but the only one who seemed to give them a welcoming smile was Gage, who also walked towards them and shook their hands. He had a very warm smile, dark brown hair, and light blue eyes; it was a very appeasing combination. Pam glared at him before continuing.

"They will all be participating in your training. Now if you will follow me over to the mats."

"So do we get cool uniforms?" Chad asked watching Pam walking over to the mats.

Pam looked at them and gave a snort of disgust. "No," she told them with no further explanation. "Now if we could continue without any further interruptions," she said with that same tone, implying that any time they opened their mouth they were wasting her precious time.

"What she means to say is that these are the uniforms for the Alpha team. Each team here at the Command Center has their own uniforms," Gage told them in an undertone trying to smooth out the tension that Pam seemed to be trying to send their way.

"So what team are we part of?" Chad asked.

"None." Pam's look turned even harder if that was possible. "Let's get one thing straight here. I don't care that you are the Guardians and have all these 'Nifty' little powers." She even used her fingers to make quote marks. "I'm not here to fawn all over you, bow down to you, nor do I care about making sure you are happy and enjoying yourself."

Well, that is obvious. Telara bit her tongue from speaking out loud.

"Didn't realize that being friendly was a crime," Chance muttered.

Pam ignored him. "I am here to train you all, and that is what I am going to do, although your training should have started long before now." The implication that they were the ones who were inconveniencing her was loud and clear.

Gage opened his mouth to speak, whether to agree with Pam or come to their defense they would never know as Pam held up her hand to silence him.

"But no matter. I have had worse to deal with although I can't remember when."

Tia gave Telara a puzzled look. After all, Pam didn't look much older than them, but the way she talked it was as if she was a veteran here. "You guys might take more work, but we will at least make you somewhat acceptable."

Telara could handle this dressing down no longer. "So is this what they consider crystal training, making pretty little speeches rather than getting off your ass and actually doing something?"

The Alpha faction sucked in their breaths, waiting for their leader's response to such blatant disrespect. Apparently, their leader didn't get much dressing down herself, even if it was needed. Telara watched Pam purse her lips together so tightly they almost disappeared, her white skin going pink in her anger. Telara knew to anger Pam probably wasn't the smartest thing to do, especially as she was the one in charge of their so-called crystal training, whatever that meant.

"Fine, you want me to do something?" Pam asked sweetly – *too sweetly*, Telara thought. "Gage, go grab the training staffs for our resident heroes."

"Ummmm.....Pam shouldn't we..."

Pam interrupted him and screeched, "I don't care what was said! Get me the staffs! Let's see if their moves are as quick as their mouths."

After giving what sounded like a heavy sigh, Gage came back with wooden staffs for all of them. They noticed the Alpha faction all had staffs also, although theirs looked more sturdy and cooler than their plain wooden staffs.

Telara held up her wooden staff. "What does this have to do with crystals?"

Pam smirked at her. "Oh I'm so sorry; I didn't realize that training with the big boys was too much for you." Pam straightened out of her offensive stance. It seemed everyone here had the physique of a warrior, except for them. "I guess we will just have to tone it down for you seven."

"Bring it!" Telara knew she was being baited, but she still saw red. She was sure this was in retaliation for her interrupting Pam's great speech. She figured after all the training they had with Raphael they at least had a fighting chance. She was wrong.

Within the hour, they found themselves on their backs more times than they could count and had many bruises they could already feel forming. After Pam knocked Tia down for the tenth time, Tia jumped back up feeling the frustration building along with anger that this training was more like a beating than anything else. When Tia swung the staff with all her frustration, they felt the air start to crackle and then they saw Pam lift off her feet and fly several feet before landing against a mat on the opposite wall. Tia just stood there staring, not sure exactly what to do as she hadn't meant for that to happen. Before she could get out an apology, Pam stalked back over to her, wrenching the staff out of her hand.

"It seems you can't handle a simple training exercise without relying on your powers." Pam glared at Tia, her face a deep red from the anger at being bested in such a way.

Tia looked at Telara, who was staring at Pam and trying to control her anger at the unfairness of that statement. After all, everyone here was supposed to be descendants of Gods of some sort. They were here to learn how to use their powers, but Pam made out that it was a crime to do so.

Chad piped up before Telara could let her anger out through very damaging words. "I thought that was the purpose: to train our powers."

Pam gave him one of her signature looks of disdain. "I

could care less about your so-called powers; all I have to do is to teach you how to use the crystals."

Telara held up her very wooden staff "This does not look like any type of crystal to me unless it is hiding under the wood."

Gage gave a chuckle earning him a glare from Pam. Telara smiled back at him feeling a bit better that they had at least one ally here.

"If you can't handle mere mortal weapons than what makes you think you can actually handle a crystal?" This was said with much mockery. "Looks like it is remedial training for you lot."

"We don't need remedial training, but some actual training would be nice," Telara said in a very controlled tone. She could feel her body hum with the power that flowed through her and tried to calm herself before she let it loose as Tia had. Pam was watching her closely and seemed to realize that she was pushing her too far so she then told them to break for lunch.

The lunchroom was bigger than any they had ever been in, and the tables were of all different sizes and shapes. There were smaller circular tables and then larger rectangular ones, and the chairs were all padded and looked like they could actually be considered to be comfortable. The food line was a long table with pizza, hamburgers, subs, and some food that they were not sure what it was and not brave enough to try. When they had filled their trays, they followed Pam over to a small circular table in the corner that looked barely big enough to accommodate them.

"Here is your place of honor," Pam said without looking at them; then she walked over to the square table that was seated on a platform at the far end of the room from them where the others from her group sat.

"Well, at least we don't have to deal with her giving us indigestion while we eat," Cole said with a mouthful of pizza, earning him a glare from Tia. He gave her a wink, but she just looked away.

Chad snickered.

"What?" They looked at him unsure what he thought was so funny.

Chad leaned back in his seat grinning as he looked over at the table where Raven sat looking as if she was holding court with her head held at a regal posture. "The Grinch hated Christmas! The whole Christmas season!" He spoke, still staring at Pam, his voice taking on an announcer tone. "Now, please don't ask why. No one quite knows the reason. It could be her head wasn't screwed on just right. It could be, perhaps, that her ponytail was just too tight. But I think that the most likely reason of all may have been that her rubber band holding her hair was two sizes too small."

The table burst out in laughter when they realized Chad had been quoting Dr. Suess, drawing curious glances from all around the room and of course a glare from the royal Grinch sitting at her table. They didn't care though; it felt good to laugh after the training session today.

"Why do I get the feeling that we have just been allocated to the unpopular table?" Vanna asked, shaking her head.

"I would say that is a very accurate description," I.Q. said, eating his food.

"Hi, guys." A very perturbed Gage walked over with his tray in hand.

Telara smiled up at him. "Hi! I would offer you a seat, but there is barely enough room for us here," she said with a grimace.

He smiled slightly at her. "Look guys, I am really sorry

about the way Pam is being with you. She isn't usually so…" He paused as if trying to come up with a word to describe her behavior.

"Rude," Telara supplied for him.

"Belligerent," Tia said with a smile.

"Insulting," Chad said leaning back in his chair.

"Abrasive," Gage finished looking a bit more uncomfortable than when he first had.

"Not your fault," Telara told him. "I guess we just rub her the wrong way."

"There is actually a bit more to it," he said slowly and very sheepishly. Then, as Pam hollered his name, he gave them an apologetic look and ambled over towards the table to a very irritated looking Captain who glared right at Telara.

"Welcome to the Sanctuary," Telara grumbled then picked at her food; her appetite seeming to disappear.

After lunch, they met with Lucius in the courtyard, and he escorted them back to the training fields where Raphael waited for them. Lucius then told them he would see them after dinner; he had something he wanted to show them.

"So how was your training with Pam?" Raphael asked them.

"Very enlightening," Telara supplied sitting on the picnic table.

"Pam can be a bit overwhelming I agree, but she is the best at the Command Center, and all of you could learn much from her."

They just mumbled and, with a quizzical glance at them, he then proceeded to their training. They ran around the field, up the path, jumping over obstacles that would suddenly appear out of nowhere, and climbed over the rocky walls that were part of their obstacle course. After they managed to actually get through the obstacle course within the time frame that Raphael wanted, he had them practice their jumps and kicks on the wooden dummies. By the time Raphael declared it was time for dinner, they had all managed to be able to block the blows from the dummies and even deliver a few of their own.

"Tomorrow, we will begin our staff training," he called to them, eliciting groans from them. He shook his head and started picking up the field.

"Man, I feel as if my bruises have bruises," Cole groaned sitting down on one of the chairs in their common room while they waited for Lucius. They didn't have long to wait as Lucius walked in and announced they were to follow him. Lucius was wearing jeans and another button-down shirt, looking relaxed and making them all jealous; there was nothing relaxing about their day.

They went down the hallway that led up to Tia's and I.Q.'s rooms then down another hallway walking past Cole's and Chad's rooms. Next, they went down several flights of steps before they came to a stone wall. If not for earlier at the Command Center they would have believed that they had hit a dead end, but they noticed the crystal on the wall. This crystal kept changing not only its shape but its color. It was a red flame, a blue teardrop, a silver wave, a white crystal, a green leaf, a bright yellow lightning bolt, and then a clear ball. Lucius turned to them and told them to walk up to the crystal and, when they felt the pull, to touch the crystal then step back. Cole walked up when the crystal became a red flame and grasped it, causing the crystal to glow brightly and the room to warm up. A blue teardrop caused Chance to reach out, and they felt a mist of water. When it was a silver wave, Tia grasped it, and they felt air caress their cheeks. Chad touched a white crystal, bringing an icy mist around the crystal. When it was a green leaf, Vanna grasped it, and they saw the vines move around the walls. I.Q. touched a yellow lightning bolt, and they felt the electricity and their hair all stood on end eliciting a giggle from the girls. When it turned to a clear ball, Telara then felt the pull deep down in her gut. She grasped the crystal and felt the energy pulse through her body and suddenly could hear her friends' thoughts as if they were her own. She released the crystal and jumped back as the wall fell away.

8

____

"W-o-w!" Chance breathed staring at the sight laid out in front of them. Telara also felt very stunned at the beauty of the world in front of them: a world of green grass and trees, blue water and sky. They were inside a mountain; yet, right there in front of them stood the most beautiful landscape any of them had ever seen. Not even a Monet painting could compete.

"Are we out of the mountain?" Vanna asked watching a butterfly flutter right by her.

"No, this piece of heaven is protected inside the mountain that surrounds all of Sanctuary," Lucius informed them.

"What is this place called?" Telara asked stepping further into this new world. She was mesmerized by what she was seeing. The sky seemed to go on forever; she could not see any evidence of the mountain except for where they had entered until she looked to her right. There, she saw along the mountain wall what looked to her to be a library with books along the walls and chairs that were made out of wood with cushions that actually had colors. On a wooden table in the center of the room was a computer monitor, but there was no tower, keyboard, or mouse. On another table, there was what looked like a radio with dials and buttons.

She looked back at Lucius, who smiled and answered her question. "This place has had many names over the years but, for now, just consider this to be your very own part of Sanctuary."

"I'm surprised others don't want to come down here; it feels so peaceful and relaxing," Vanna said finding a nice seat by the closest tree.

"If they knew of it, they probably would," Lucius told them.

"No one knows of this place?" Tia asked, surprised how anyone would be able to keep this magnificent place hidden.

Lucius chuckled. "The magic of this place is even stronger than that of the Sanctuary above ground. The only ones that are able to access this room are the ones who can harness the power. The ones who came before you used this room to relax and practice their powers where they had privacy and couldn't harm others in the process."

Tia felt a bit uncomfortable. She was not sure if he already knew about her outburst at the Command Center.

"Here, you will be able to unwind from your day and hopefully learn to control the power that is a part of you. This place was created to be able to relax and meditate away from others. Maybe you can use it as your own training room," Lucius suggested.

"What do you mean the ones who came before us?" Telara asked, knowing that the answer was very significant to them.

"You're not the first group that has come to Sanctuary whose powers manifest themselves a little more prominently than others." Lucius smiled at them, as if that one statement should make complete sense to them. The peaceful feeling that

Telara experienced upon first entering this room was fast disappearing. Lucius' comments that seemed to explain everything and yet nothing at all were grating against her nerves.

"But why? If we can use our powers without the crystals, why should we even bother with them?" The idea of no more training with Pam prompted Telara to ask this question.

"Because while they are just an extension, they also help to control and amplify your powers in ways you could never imagine unless you experience it. There is so much more to tell you but until you are ready, I can't."

"When will we know when we are ready?" Tia asked.

"When you don't have to ask," they were informed.

Telara jerked as if she had just been poked in the back. It was a very short sentence, and as cryptic as all the others Lucius had said many times, but the feelings she felt from that one statement were intense: sadness, guilt, and a very strong yearning. Sadness and guilt over the situation they were in? Over not being able to tell them everything? A yearning to tell them more? Telara was not sure, but she was beginning to think there was more to Lucius than they were seeing.

"Hey, the power ball is here," Chad said picking up the ball, The frosty film again covered the ball. He threw it to Chance who, in turn, threw the now ball of water to Cole causing the ball to steam up then turn fire red.

"This is where the ball has always belonged; however, when Raphael discovered it among his equipment, we decided to try to see if it would help you with your powers. It seems the ball just wanted to come home," Lucius chuckled.

"Are you saying the ball is actually alive?" Vanna asked.

"I don't know myself, as it does not do anything for me, but sit there. That is something you will have to discover for yourselves." With that said, he turned to walk out of the room.

"Hey," Telara said, causing him to turn to her. "You are just going to leave?" she asked him, earning her some curious looks. She had not shown one iota of liking Lucius and now she was acting as if she wanted him to stay.

"I am only the Caretaker here," he told her, giving her a smile as if unaware of the looks she was receiving from her friends. "You will have to work on your powers yourself; I have done as much as I can for you at the present time. You will be able to find me when needed."

"How? We don't know where you go when you leave us," Telara said.

"As I said, when needed you will be able to find me. Now go and enjoy your freedom. When you are ready to leave, you will be able to find your way," he said. Then, he disappeared through the wall.

"Thought you didn't like him?" Tia asked her. The others looked just as curious about that.

Telara shrugged. "I can't tell you how, but I can tell you that I know he was sincere in what he said. I could feel that he really wanted to tell us more but, for whatever reason, he couldn't." Telara grabbed a book off the shelf. "I trust him." She didn't look at them but sat down in a chair and opened the book.

"Hmmm…" I.Q. murmured.

"What?" Cole asked him.

"What Telara just described is the power of an empath."

"Or it could just be women's intuition," Vanna told them. "Not everything has to deal with powers you know." They chuckled about that, considering that should have been an argument from I.Q. rather than anyone else. It seemed this place was affecting all of them.

They looked back over at their new area. Chance looked at

the river and, within minutes, was down to his swim trunks and dove in. They smiled at that and then Vanna walked over to the trees. They watched as squirrels came out of their hiding spot and sat on her shoulder for a ride. It was said that she had the power of Mother Nature so seeing her with a critter on her shoulder was nothing new to them. Chad walked over to a wading pool and took off his socks and shoes before wading into it. Cole did the same but jumped out almost immediately, exclaiming how cold the water was. I.Q. walked over to the bookshelves, joining Telara, and grabbed a book to read. They watched as the radio seemed to come alive as he walked by it, and they heard the tunes of their favorite band. Tia went and sat next to Vanna, watching Chance come up for air after several minutes under.

While it didn't seem as if there was much of a difference here than anywhere else when it came to their powers, it was definitely a very peaceful place. Telara noticed a book on one of the tables next to her that had some strange markings on the cover. She opened the book, but all she saw was more shapes and weird-looking markings.

It must be some type of ancient language, she thought.

"Here, let me see," I.Q. said to her.

"Huh?" She looked at him.

"Let me look. I can tell you if it is some ancient language," he said to her.

"You heard me?" she asked.

"Yeah, why wouldn't I?" he asked.

"No reason." Telara shrugged and then thought of something.

Can you hear me? she asked in her mind. *If you can, don't answer with your mouth but your mind,* she said as an idea occurred to her.

Yes, I can hear you.

"I heard you," Telara said excitedly.

The others came over to see what the excitement was all about. Telara and I.Q. told them what they had found out, so they sat there and started talking with their minds. "Mind Speaking" was what Vanna called it, and they thought that sounded about right.

Just like Telara and her dream walking, Cole thought, laughing in his mind.

They sat there mind talking for over an hour before they seemed to get sleepy, and the book lay forgotten on the small table over by the red cushioned chair. They went to bed and decided they would see how far they could get before they could no longer mind talk. It seemed like the further they got away, the lower their voices were until they could no longer hear one another. Telara smiled to herself as she felt herself drift off to sleep that night to her little friends playing on the ceiling.

That night, Telara again had the dream with the Shadows reaching for her and blocking out the light, taking away all her senses. She started to shake and tried to calm her nerves, refusing to let the darkness win.

Again, that voice called out to her, "Katharisete to myalo sas pyrotechnima."

She still didn't understand what he was saying, but this time she could feel the encouragement from the voice. In addition, she wasn't sure how she knew it, but she knew he was trying to show her that he believed in her.

"Tora antepitethoun."

"Yes, time to fight back." Telara was sure that was what was being said even though she didn't understand him.

"Chrisimopoilsei ti dynami sas."

Telara reached out with her mind into the darkness and felt the malevolence from the Shadows, but she also felt something else. She felt the light from Cole, who was sleeping soundly on the other side of Sanctuary.

"Daneizetai tin exousia."

Telara felt her body start to glow and, although she wasn't sure how, she focused her might on that glow to keep it growing. She saw the Shadows recoil from her as if they were being burned and then disappear. She felt the anger from the Shadows as well as the satisfaction from Bright Eyes.

"Evge."

She turned and saw Bright Eyes standing by the tree, smiling at her with that smile of his that made her heart flutter even though she knew he could be a ghost. Then again, she had never seen a ghost as cute as this one. He definitely had the bad boy grin down to go along with his dark hair and eyes, not to mention the one little lock of hair that fell over his forehead. She started to walk towards him but, with one last smile, he slowly faded away.

"No, don't go!" she shouted, but he was already gone. She was disappointed that she didn't get to thank him but felt great elation at her victory.

She looked around and shouted, "I did it! I defeated the Shadows."

Closing her eyes, she tipped her head back and when she opened her eyes next, she was staring at her circles and lines racing across the ceiling as if they were celebrating for her.

9

———

Tᴵᴬ ʟᴏᴏᴋᴇᴅ ᴏᴠᴇʀ ᴀᴛ Tᴇʟᴀʀᴀ, who was also lying on the mat propped up by her elbows after being knocked down by Pam for the sixth time that day. Pam stood there smiling down at Telara, who had to calm herself down before she sent the irritating commander across the room or hung her from the ceiling by her ponytail. The past few days seemed to settle into a routine of getting knocked around during the training with Pam and her comrades; the only one who took any pity on them and actually tried to help them was Gage. The rest seemed to take delight in showing them that they were superior to them. Between Raphael's teaching and the abuse they were taking here, they ended very sore and tired by the time they got to relax in the Static Room, as they had come to call their room. That had become their favorite time of day. They were able to relax without someone breathing down their necks regarding powers that barely worked or someone doing their best to make them feel less than they were. Their mind speaking, as they had come to call it, was the only power that seemed to come easy to them.

After the beatings they took at the Command Center, they would spend their time in the Static Room, where Lucius found them and commented on how tired they were.

"Your training with Raphael should not cause you to be this tired," he said, watching them with concern.

"Well, gee, let's not count the beating we take at the Command Center," Vanna muttered. The training with Pam and her crew was starting to make her more and more irritated as well.

"Beating?" Lucius asked. "Training with the crystals should not be considered a beating."

"Crystals?" Tia asked. "What are you talking about crystals? All we do is go there while they knock us down on our backside then smile and tell us that we are not trying hard enough."

"You should not be doing any combat training with them. That is what Raphael is teaching you. I only required them to show you how to work the crystals, which I expected to be done soon," Lucius said, appearing to be perturbed over this new information. "I will have to speak to Ira; the orders must have gotten crossed somewhere."

"You mean to say that all they are supposed to be showing us is how to use the crystals?" Telara asked, her temper starting to show. "And instead they keep knocking us down with staffs, nunchucks, and plain old hand-to-hand combat?"

"I am sure that they just misunderstood," Lucius said in a thoughtful tone, but Telara was having none of that.

"I bet."

She looked over at the others who were nodding with her.

"I will discuss this with Ira and get it rectified," he said, going to walk out the door.

"Wait!"

Lucius came to an abrupt halt and turned his head slowly to give Telara a very startled look. Not one of them could blame him for his trepidation. After all, Telara had given him nothing but grief since they had first come here.

"Pam keeps talking about preparing us for battle. What is she talking about?" Telara had to ask before she lost her nerve.

They had been discussing this amongst themselves but now Telara wanted more answers than they had. When Lucius looked as if he was going to leave without an answer, Telara continued,

"No one has a Command Center with the Intel that we have seen here to just teach a bunch of kids about their ancestry. Maybe Sanctuary is for learning powers and to protect all the mythical beings here, but there is more to the Command Center than that….isn't there?"

Lucius gave a deep sigh before answering as if to come up with the right words. "The Command Center is not only tasked with keeping our worlds separated but also to protect our world and the outside world from the darkness that threatens us all."

"What is the darkness?" Chance asked, abandoning his water time antics to get in on this discussion.

Telara thought about her dreams and the Shadows. She shivered remembering how helpless she had first felt. She had really hoped that those nightmares were just that and not some sign of what was ahead of them. Defeating the Shadows in her dream was one thing but to have to face them in real life was not something she was not looking forward to.

"The darkness is exactly that – darkness. Creatures that are just pure evil. They are as dark as a starless night, and their souls are as bleak. There are many different types of these soulless creatures, but the main ones that we come into contact with are called Shadow Minions. They are the most abundant of all the Shadow creatures, and all of them are controlled by the Shadow Master."

"Why don't you just take out the Shadow Master? You have to have enough firepower here to do just that," Cole said, playing with a small flame in his hand as he was talking. Vanna was watching that flame very closely, considering the first time Cole had conjured a flame in his hand, he had dropped it right onto the ground and caught some nearby leaves on fire. If not for Chance, they might have had a bit of a problem.

Lucius gave them a sad smile. "If only it was that simple. The minions are not the only creatures that the Shadow Master commands and while the others are not as abundant, they are more lethal. Those are the ones the Shadow Master uses to protect himself. Many of the Command Center troops have lost their lives trying to do just that." Lucius seemed even sadder than before after that comment which caused Telara to feel bad for bringing it up.

"Why is it we don't see more people using their powers around Sanctuary? As a matter of fact, I haven't seen one person here show any sign of magical power."

Lucius seemed to visually stiffen at Telara's question. There was such a long pause that Telara was sure he was going to ignore the question altogether.

"I am afraid that when it comes to bestowing the gift of magic, the Gods do not grant it to all of their descendants. As a matter of fact, you seven are the only known ones with such a gift right now."

Telara looked at each of her friends as understanding seemed to creep in. "You mean we are the only ones here with power like ours?"

Lucius nodded. "That is correct, but I would be careful in announcing that around Sanctuary; while it is common knowledge, there are still some who feel cheated as such."

Telara nodded. She could think of one person in particular who would feel cheated and right now, she was torn between wanting to rub Pam's nose in it or trying to keep the peace. The former would give her more satisfaction, but the latter would probably be smarter.

"Do you really have to say something to Ira?" She didn't want to think about Pam's reaction to that.

Lucius looked at Telara and frowned. "Yes, I do. I need you all to know how to use the crystals; otherwise, there is no reason for you to be here. Raphael can teach you any fighting technique there is but even he cannot use a crystal. Only the descendants have the power to use a crystal weapon."

"I wouldn't mind giving up enhanced powers; I like our powers the way they are," Cole said sullenly. None of them were interested in having more to do with Pam or her troop.

"Those Shadow creatures I told you about, they are attracted to power." He looked up at them. "Power like yours. Their master believes that collecting others' powers will help him to take over and rule. If they were to catch a whiff of your powers, you would find yourself in a very bad situation. The crystals are the only way to do any damage to them. Without them, you would be a sitting duck." He held up his hand at their protests and continued. "Now, tomorrow, I will see to it that Pam will start your crystal training immediately. Without that training, you will not be prepared to defend yourselves against the Shadow creatures. Your powers are not even close to being strong enough to protect yourselves."

That being said, he walked out and left them to their maudlin thoughts. None were too thrilled with the coming of morning. They were sure that Pam would make them regret taking away her fun.

Sure enough, the following morning Pam met them in the entryway with a very disgruntled look and a very contrite looking Gage. Without saying a word, she motioned for them to follow her. She took them to another wing in the Command Center and into a small room where there was a table with crystal wands that had silver handles.

She motioned for them to grab one and said, with a look of disdain on her face, "Apparently, our honored guests couldn't handle the training of warriors, so we have been instructed to take it easy and instead instruct them on how to use the crystals." She turned towards them. "Let's hope that you will be able to take to using the crystals better than you have taken to combat. If not, I'm sure we will be around to save you."

Yeah, and if that happens, I am sure we will never hear the end of it, Telara thought to her friends, who all agreed with a grimace. This exchange did not go unnoticed by Gage, who gave all of them inquiring looks. They just smiled at him, not ready to reveal their form of communication to anyone else just yet, even their only friend here at the Command Center.

"Grab a belt from the wall also," Gage told them gesturing to the leather belts that were hanging from hooks on the other side of the room. "The metal from the crystals will attach itself to the belt automatically. This makes it so that it is easily accessible and yet there are no worries of misplacing your crystal."

"After all, even your powers can't help to locate a missing crystal," Pam said glaring at Gage. They were amazed at how much Gage would try to help him even though it had to earn him many reprimands from Pam who wanted them to get as little help as possible. They wanted to scream at her that it was not their fault that they had powers while she did not but, then again, they agreed that it would probably make their situation worse.

They just smiled at him and followed Pam out of the room into another large room where they saw dummies on the other side of the wall.

"Your goal is to use your crystals to knock over the dummies on the other side," Pam said. She grasped her wand and with a flick, they watched one of the dummies fall to the ground. "Not too hard," she said with a smile then sat down in a chair and motioned for them to start.

Okay, so what do we do? Cole looked at them.

Um, I guess we point the crystals like she did and concentrate on knocking the dummies over, Tia said pointing her crystal at the dummy nearest her.

She grasped her crystal tight as she flicked her hand. They felt the air rush from the wand in her hand and saw the dummy fly back several feet but stay upright. Pam just smirked causing Tia to concentrate even harder to knock over the dummy. Unfortunately, all she accomplished was pushing it firmly against the far wall. Cole tried but was unsuccessful in even moving the dummy. In a fit of frustration, he managed to cause a jet of fire to shoot across the room, burning the dummy where it stood until there was only the stand left. Pam and her team jumped up and glared at him.

"The object is to knock it over without destroying it," she said with a glare. "I see you still do not have control of your powers. Great, let's just release a bunch of untrained children into the world," she grumbled, glaring at them.

Vanna could not get her crystal wand to do much other than give a green glow. Chance shot water out, which managed to spray all over Pam and her faction. Telara and her friends chuckled over that while Pam seemed to glare even more, if that was possible. Chad's wand just iced over. I.Q.'s sent out sparks that reminded them of fireworks which amused them but not Pam and her crew. Well, unless you counted Gage, who seemed to have a hard time holding back his grin. Telara found herself wishing that Gage was the commander of this group rather than just Pam's second in command. Finally, it seemed to be Telara's turn. She grasped her crystal by the silver handle. She looked over at the dummy in front of her and pointed her wand towards the dummy. She concentrated on that dummy and imagined the dummy falling over. She flicked her crystal and watched as the dummy start to sway then land on its side. Her friends cheered as she had done what they had not been able to do and what Pam didn't think they could do.

"Was that from the crystal or did you use your own powers?" Pam asked in an irritated voice.

Telara wasn't sure if she knew how to talk to them as if they were actual people rather than a nuisance she was saddled with.

"The object of this training is to use the power of the crystals not yours," Pam informed them.

"You wanted the dummy knocked over and lo and behold the dummy is on its side," Tia told her just as snidely.

Pam harrumphed and told them it was time to start the next exercise. This was to create a stream of light from the crystals. None of them seemed to able to do this, causing Pam to start smiling again and her gloating comments to start yet again. The rest of the day until lunch it seemed Pam was intent on giving them exercises that she felt they would not be able to do.

"Do you get the feeling she is setting us up to fail?" Cole asked them after their attempt to use their crystals to turn a crooked rock into a smooth round rock had failed. "I mean, have you noticed they have not used their crystals once since Pam did the first exercise with the dummy?"

"They don't need to; we are the novices here," Vanna muttered still trying to smooth out the surface of the rock.

"And, at this rate, I don't see that changing," Telara said getting more and more frustrated with these exercises.

They were happy to be breaking up for lunch and actually felt more energetic this time when they would train with Raphael. They found it very helpful to exercise their frustrations out on the dummies he had set up and, within the week, while they had not had better luck with the crystals they could do the obstacle course and take down a dummy without tiring themselves out like before.

One evening, in the Static Room, Vanna discovered a new friend: a silver squirrel that Chance had named Streak. He called him this because, once, when Streak was startled, he took up the tree, and Chance swore all he saw was a silver streak. They never saw Streak outside the Static Room but as soon as they entered, he would be perched on Vanna's shoulder, and there he would stay until they left.

The other discovery they had made in the Static Room was the Stargazer. While searching through the bookshelves one evening, Telara had come across a flat purple and black box that resembled a slim-line laptop such as they had back home. I.Q. took hold of it and, with one touch, the top flipped up to reveal a keypad and screen. The keypad had no letters or numbers that they could recognize, but I.Q. had it fired up within minutes and was busy tapping away trying to discover the laptop's secrets. On the screen, it looked as if there were millions of stars twinkling at them.

"Stargazer." I.Q. looked up at Tia and smiled at her with a nod. "It fits."

The Stargazer became almost an obsession with I.Q. Every chance he got, he was tapping away trying to figure it out. He had taken it out and was tapping away when Lucius walked into the common room one evening. I.Q. hurriedly hid it behind his back, and Lucius left without a word about the Stargazer. After Lucius had gone, they discovered why he hadn't said anything; the Stargazer had shrunk and was now the size of a CD.

"Cool!" Cole was the first to break the silence. "I want one of those; it would come handy in school. I could read whatever magazine I wanted and when the teacher gets close...POOF...it would just shrink, and I could hide it without being caught."

I.Q. shook his head at him, opened the Stargazer back to its original size, and went back to tapping away.

Tia was still unable to conjure up more than a gust of wind, but she did try. Chance was able to create small waves in the pond. Chad was so excited when he was able to create a thin layer of ice over the small wading pool that he fell in and broke the ice. Cole found he was able to create a flame in his hand but every time he tried to make it larger, it would go out. Vanna discovered once that she was able to move the limbs on a tree; Chance helped with that when he accidentally sent a wave towards her to which the tree blocked most of the water. I.Q. found it easy to manipulate the radio without even going near it, so they always had music playing through the Static Room. Telara had upgraded from just opening books to actually levitating one from the bookshelf into her hands.

While these seemed like small achievements; to them, it was as if they had already conquered the world. Their powers were not as strong by themselves as they were when they used the power ball, but they were still progressing. The only time they felt as if they had failed was at the Command Center with Pam and her crew. They had hoped that when it came time for them to actually fight, it would be with some other team, but they were soon to be very disappointed.

10

THEY HAD JUST FINISHED their lunch after their brutal match with Pam and her crew. Heading towards Raphael and his obstacle course that they could now get through without breaking a sweat, they were in good spirits. Cole had just shoved Chad when they heard sirens and saw lights flashing. They looked over at Cole, who shrugged his shoulder as if to say, "It wasn't me."

A guy in a white coat rushed past them only stopping when Telara hollered out to him.

"What's going on?" she asked him. He looked at her as if she had sprouted another head. She bit her tongue as they were all getting sick of how the people of the Command Center seemed to regard them as something to be wary of rather than just normal people.

"Don't you see the purple lights and hear the sirens?" he asked incredulously.

Telara got the feeling this was another of the items that Pam was obligated to inform them of and was sure it had conveniently slipped her mind.

"Shadow attack! Better get to the Command Room immediately."

"Command Room? Where is that?" Vanna asked, but the man had already disappeared through one of the frosted doors. Telara and the others just looked at each other than at the many doors that were around them. Which one led into the Command Room and how many doors would they have to go through to get there? Sometimes, this place was more a maze than any cornfield they had ever been in. They knew how to get to the foyer where they stood and how to get from the cafeteria back to the fields.

"There you are."

They turned their heads and felt a surge of relief as they saw Lucius coming their way. He smiled at them and put his hand on Telara's shoulder.

"A Shadow attack outside of the Sanctuary. I need to know if you guys feel ready to take on some Shadow Minions," he said as kindly as possible considering the circumstances.

They glanced nervously at each other; they couldn't even get their crystals to do what Pam kept telling them they could do, let alone actually do battle. Their powers themselves, while they seemed to come a bit easier, were still a puzzle to them at times. Their hands were suddenly sweaty and their mouths dry.

"You will not be on your own," Lucius was quick to assure them noticing the looks on all their faces. When that didn't seem to ease their strained faces, he went on to say, "Better to face them when you will at least have some help." They saw the sense behind that statement and reluctantly nodded their heads. "Exterior defense is run by Carmen of the Beta group and while she is not as seasoned as Pam, I am sure you will still flourish as well with her teaching in the field."

"You mean we won't be going with Pam and the Alpha group?" Chad asked, perking up.

"Not for exterior defense," Lucius said as if that was something that everyone here knew.

Most likely everyone here but us does know, Telara thought.

Not being able to mind speak, Lucius continued on. "Come on, let's put your training to the test." This was said with a grin as if he believed they would do more than just fine.

They followed him to the same room in which they had first met Pam and Ira. This time, there was not a single terminal that didn't have a person there typing furiously away. The tap-tapping of the keys echoed through the room; there was limited conversation, allowing the sound to echo all around. I.Q. made a comment on how those normal-looking computers just did not look right here.

"Yeah, crystal balls definitely would fit in more accurately," Chad said, looking up at the screen that dominated the front of the room.

The images of people running and screaming through sunlit streets were what blared out to them this time. In one image, they saw an evil-looking creature that was as dark as night. The sharp pointed teeth shined brightly and very viciously from the angled face. They shivered at the image.

Lucius chuckled. "Yes, computers but not ones like you know, nor are they powered the way you are used to."

With that said, he pointed over to the far wall where wires were running up the walls and joined at one spot on the wall. There, they saw a jagged-looking crystal that was shining brightly. They did not see any certain color coming from the crystal; it seemed to shine as if it was a light fixture, but they knew that it was not.

"Does that make up for the lack of crystal balls?"

Chad looked down at his feet and didn't respond to that comment. Lucius just chuckled.

"Come on, let's get you guys ready for your first assignment."

They pulled their gaze from the frightening image on the screen and followed him.

Lucius took them up to the landing where Ira stood talking with Pam. She was dressed in her normal black jumpsuit, but there seemed to be some additions. Around her waist was a utility belt almost like the ones you see on the movie superheroes, but hers had crystals all hanging down in different colors. All the crystals were no bigger than a quarter. Hooked to her belt was the crystal that they always saw her with during training. Her belt definitely looked grandeur than their simple brown leather straps they wore around their waists. She had never let them use the same crystal twice stating that they needed to learn to be able to adjust. Which never happened; it seemed as soon as they got used to the one they were using, they had to start all over again the next day.

Pam broke off what she was saying to Ira and glared when she noticed who it was with Lucius.

"Hello Ira," Lucius said, smiling and nodding towards him then turned towards Pam. He seemed to be unaware of the dirty looks she was sending to Telara and them.

"Pam," he smiled.

"Exactly what are they doing here?" Pam asked with a slight sneer at them and then she smiled up at Lucius with what Telara could only describe as a pageant smile: very fake.

"They are here to assist Carmen and her team of course," Lucius said matter-of-factly. He turned back to Ira only to be interrupted by Pam.

"Carmen and her team are in the middle of their Los

Angeles assignment and have yet to return. Alpha team will be taking care of our little minion problem today," Pam informed him.

Lucius' smile never dropped at hearing this news. They hoped that maybe Lucius would just pull them out after hearing this bit of news, but their hopes were dashed with his next words.

"Well then, I guess you and your team will benefit from their training."

"They can't even do remedial exercises with their crystals let alone do battle with them," she said looking at Lucius as if he had gone mad.

"If their crystal training had started when it was supposed to we might not even be having this issue," Lucius said in a polite, but pointed, manner causing Pam to glance away from him and reaffirming their suspicions that it was purposely done. His icy blue eyes pinned the Alpha captain, and they could have sworn that her pony tail drooped under his stare.

"Be that as it may," Lucius continued as if he did not notice Pam's sudden discomfort. "I am sure under your leadership, since you are the best the Command Center has, they will do fine in battle and maybe learn something. Unless, of course, you are telling me that you are not up to the task. If so, you should have informed me sooner, and we could have found a suitable replacement." This was said in a more pointed manner and even Telara felt the reprimand from Lucius.

They looked at one another. They had never heard that tone from Lucius, not even in the beginning when Telara kept giving him a hard time. Pam flushed at that but kept her lips pursed together.

Lucius said, "But since this attack is only a minion attack, I see no reason why they can't assist you, and I will look into finding a replacement afterward. Unless you can tell me of a better reason why they shouldn't assist?" Lucius asked her.

"No. No reason," Pam said tightly.

Telara was sure if she pursed her lips any harder, they would completely disappear. She seemed to do that a lot around them. Pam turned towards them.

"Make sure to follow all my directions and no showboating."

She turned away with a sharp turn and walked down the plank towards where her team stood. They were dressed in the same manner as she, along with some men and women dressed in the white coats.

"Oh, and Pam," Lucius said to her retreating back. She stopped but did not turn around. "I trust you will make sure that they do more than just sit on the sidelines."

You could see her shoulders tense as she said nothing but just kept walking. They looked at Lucius, who smiled and wished them luck. Telara was sure they were going to need more than luck.

They were fitted in suits like those that Pam wore except that theirs were a royal blue in color. They also had a headset so that they could hear orders when they were given. Pam handed them their crystals, telling them to attach them to their belts and take them off only when needed. While Pam no longer sneered at them, her attitude was no more friendly than normal. When Cole asked if they were going to get the other crystals that were hanging down from the Alpha team's belts, he was informed that they would not need them nor were they experienced enough to use them. That halted any other question they had; they decided via mind talk that that they would just listen and try not to screw up. Their crystals still felt very uncomfortable with them.

They followed the group through a door that led to a white-walled room with no windows and no furniture of any kind. It kind of reminded them of a huge elevator that had a regular main door rather than the typical elevator doors. Pam was giving everyone orders while purposely ignoring them, which, at this point, suited them just fine. The others in the room listened to Pam and seemed to have their game faces on as they no longer smiled or joked. The white coats, Cole had started to call them, were fitting their headpieces and adjusting the bags that resembled a purse you might see on a bag lady. The bags seemed to be filled with crystals that had no definite shape except for some jagged edges. They also had no specific color; rather, they looked pretty clear. On their hands, they noticed there was a leather band that looped through the fingers and wrapped around the wrist with a smooth crystal that sat in their palms. They looked at that then glanced at each other all wondering what that was for but not in the mood for any of Pam's snide comments. The room started to hum, and they could feel the vibrations in the walls. It made them feel as if they were indeed in an elevator that was moving. As the vibrations grew in intensity, the walls around them seemed to glow very brightly.

"Glasses on," Pam shouted.

However, before Telara and the other Guardians could tell them that they had no glasses to put on, the light grew even brighter, and they had to shield their eyes from the brightness. As suddenly as the light came, it was gone along with the vibrations. On the other side of the room, a door appeared. Telara was still seeing spots from the light, so she and the others stumbled out of the room behind the Alpha team and the white coats.

They were standing in a street outside of some buildings

with people screaming and running around them. It was the same street they had seen in the huge monitor. They looked around and realized they were nowhere near the Sanctuary anymore. As they turned back around where they had come from, they saw a tree and a light post. The room they had stepped out from was no longer there.

"Hey, this is the Alamo," Cole said excitedly, pointing over to the other side of the street where there was a sign proclaiming that they were indeed at the Alamo. "We are in Texas," he said excitedly.

They looked around and noticed that amidst the running and screaming tourists, they could see little dark figures reaching and grabbing for people. They were the same creatures they had seen on the monitors. The creatures' skin was darker than the darkest of night; if they were to stand in a shadow, you would not be able to see them at all. Their facial features, while somewhat human, resembled a bit of a troll. They were hunched over as if they were carrying a heavy weight on their backs, and their fingers on their hands were more like claws that looked sharp as a knife.

Vanna shrieked as one of the creatures reached for a little girl standing there clutching her doll to her chest, crying out for her mommy. One of the Alpha group, a brown-haired girl who always seemed to give them sympathetic looks during their training with them, leaped over a wooden bench and swung her crystal towards the creature. They watched as a rope of bright light formed at the end of the crystal and connected with the creature, causing it to cry out in pain and back away from the little girl, clutching at the wounded arm that seemed to be dripping a dark gooey substance.

"What are those things?" Vanna asked.

"Shadow Minions," Gage told her. "Thank the gods that

there are not that many this time," he said, looking around and holding his crystal that, to them, resembled nunchucks. In the center of the two short rods of crystal was a silver chain. The most amazing part of the crystal was that wherever he grasped it, a silver band would appear so that he never seemed to touch the crystal itself.

"Hey, where can I get one of those rather than this thing?" Cole asked holding out his crystal that still resembled a wand of sorts. Gage gave him an apologetic look and just shook his head as if to say that was not possible. Telara could feel a sense of embarrassment from Gage, but she not sure why.

"When this is over, I will have to have a talk with Pam," he told them instead and grimaced. "This animosity is ridiculous." He held up his hand as Telara went to protest. "It is nothing of your doing or anything you can control, but I think it is time I put my foot down with my leader."

"What are they doing?" I.Q. pointed to a white coat who was taking the little girl over to her mother and pressing their palms up to the sides of their heads.

"Altering their memories," Gage told them. "Those are memory crystals they carry on their hands; otherwise, everyone would know about the Shadow creatures, and there would be panic everywhere. We try to keep all this information from the outside world; no sense in everyone knowing there are Shadow creatures trying to end life as we know it," Gage chuckled. "Lucius told you that what we do at Sanctuary is kept from the outside world, didn't he?"

"Yeah, but we never really knew how or even how it all worked out," Telara said, beginning to feel as if they were pretty much kept in the dark regarding everything that mattered.

Well, that is gonna change as soon as we get back. She looked at the others who were nodding their heads in agreement. *We are supposed to be able to fight these things; yet, we know nothing. I say they either talk or we walk.*

Looking around at the chaos they were seeing, the others couldn't help but agree with that. While not wanting to add to the confrontation that would sure to be, they couldn't help but agree that this was not something they should have been thrown into like this.

"What are they doing?" Vanna asked, pointing to the other white coats that were placing the jagged-looking crystals all around the place.

"Those are illusion crystals," Gage explained. At their questioning looks, he went on to explain, "They are placed outside the area during any battle so that anyone on the outside will not see anything out of the norm. Any that try to go to cross the boundaries will feel a sudden urge to go the opposite way. That way, we can limit the number of innocents that would otherwise find themselves in harm's way. I would suggest you guys have a long talk with Lucius when this is done. It seems Pam's teachings were not the only ones that weren't as in-depth as they should be."

With that said, he left them to start clearing the area of the minions that were still trying to grab as many innocents that were within reach. He flicked his nunchucks of light at several minions. They shrieked at him; yet, they still shrunk from the light.

"I would say that is an understatement," I.Q. said looking around. He glanced back at Telara to say something but forgot what he was going to say as he saw a minion sneak towards her with a glazed look in its eyes. As the creature reached out with its claws for her, he yelled out for her to look behind her.

Telara jumped back as she saw the creature that I.Q. was

warning her about. She held up her wand hoping that it would light up as the others, but the crystal was just that: a crystal. Just as the creature reached her, a staff of light came down connecting with the creature's outreached arm. The creature gave its awful shriek and jerked back its arm but then it lunged right at her. This time, the light staff was swung so that it caught the creature in its midriff sending it flying backward and scampering off to the shadows, leaving a trail of the dark gooey substance.

"I don't have time to save you and save the actual innocents," Pam said glaring down at her and holding her staff by the silver band. "Please keep out of the way if you cannot be of any assistance."

With that said, she turned around and faced three minions that were creeping towards her. They watched as she started to twirl her staff faster and faster until it looked as if she was holding a shield of light. She started towards the creatures, chasing them off and giving the whitecoats the opportunity to get more of the innocents out of the way.

As they watched Pam, Gage, and the others from their team chase off the minions, they felt very inadequate standing there. Even the white coats were doing something productive. They looked down at their crystal wands that could not even give off a slight glow. Telara started to feel a slow anger burn inside her: anger at Pam for basically make them feel useless, anger at Lucius for not telling them all they had to expect, and anger at him giving Pam the means to discount them.

"Oh my…Telly," Vanna breathed pointing at Telara's hand.

Telara looked down and saw her crystal start to glow brightly. She looked over at Cole and saw his crystal also was shining brightly. They nodded to each other and joined in the fray, smacking any minion they could with the light wands they held. While they still felt a bit alien in their hands, the wands were still working to frighten the minions.

The creatures seemed to keep coming from everywhere and, no matter how hard they would hit one with the wands, there seemed to be another to take its place. They looked around and saw that was the case everywhere they looked. Telara remembered her dream where Cole's light helped her banish the Shadows from her dream and an idea formed. She hollered for Cole and when he neared her, she put her hand that clenched the handle of the wand against Cole's so that both the handles butted against each other. Then she watched as the handles seemed to melt right into each other until they were one. She looked at Cole and nodded. He understood, and they both concentrated all their powers on their combined crystals. They watched as the crystals burned even brighter and heard the shrieks coming from the minions that came in contact with the light.

"Keep it up," Vanna hollered. "They're retreating."

The light seemed to expand from them to reach out and attach to any minion that came close. They watched as some of the minions that could not run as fast seemed to melt right before their eyes. Telara started to feel a certain pride that she was doing what Pam could not. While Pam chased away a few, Cole and she were chasing away many and, in the process, actually destroying ones that were not fast enough.

She could vaguely hear Pam above the noise of the shrieking creatures and other yells as the light blinded several others that had looked to see what the minions were running from. Pam yelled at them to stop whatever they were doing, but Telara was having none of that. As far as Telara was concerned, Pam was just jealous that they were having the success that they were. And she was not going to let Pam take that away from her.

The light grew even brighter, so much so that Telara could not see in front of her and when she looked down at her hands, she could not see them. Suddenly, Telara lost her grip on the wands as she was knocked onto the ground. She looked up to see a very irate Pam glaring at her. Pam's dark eyes were practically glowing in her anger.

"What do you think you were doing?" she yelled at her.

Before Telara could gloat over her success, they heard someone yell out and looked over in time to see one of the minions that remained grab Gage and pull him into the shadows.

"NO!" Pam screamed and ran over to where, just a second before, Gage had stood, but it was too late. Gage was gone, along with all the other minions who seemed to disappear into the shadows.

Telara stood there and stared at the place where the creature and Gage and disappeared. *Not Gage*, Telara thought. *Anyone but him; he was the only one who seemed to be on their side, and he was the one who was taken because she had gotten a big ego and let her power get out of hand.*

She could not stop the feeling of self-loathing that was creeping into her being.

"This is entirely your fault," Pam screamed at her, tears streaming down her cheeks.

The brown-haired girl tried to calm her down, but she was having none of that. "You just had to show off didn't you? Can't be part of team? No, you have to go and show everyone how powerful you are. Well, I hope you are happy with yourself; Gage is the one to pay the price for YOUR mistake."

"That is not fair, Pam," said a white coat who was handing

a child to her mother. She motioned for another to come and modify the memories. She turned back to Pam. "We all know the stakes when we go into the field for battle."

Pam glared at her and told her to finish the cleanup because she needed to head back to the Command Center to file the report. With one last hateful look at Telara, she turned around and walked away. Telara and the others followed her without saying a word. Telara could feel the guilt eating away at her, and her friends didn't know what they could say to ease her pain.

11

———

TELARA LEFT the Command Center as quickly as she could. The angry remarks that Pam kept shooting her way were starting to take a toll. She already felt guilty as it was, and Pam kept rubbing salt in the wound. As she walked through the Command Center, she swore she could feel everyone watching her, condemning her as Pam had done. Her friends tried to talk to her, but this wasn't something they could help with, so they stayed back and just watched her. Telara could even feel her friends' apprehension as they watched her with eyes filled with sympathy. But that was not what she wanted. What she wanted was a way to fix this mess she had gotten everyone into. She kept walking at a fast pace as if the faster she walked, the farther she would get away from the problem. She knew that was futile as her mind would not let her forget the look of horror on Gage's face as he was grabbed by one of the minions right before he disappeared. Then there was the look on Pam's face as she screamed at Telara, blaming her for his capture.

Her friends followed her to the lake where Telara sat down

and leaned up against their tree that they would sit under after a day with Raphael. They tried telling her that it wasn't her fault; that she was only trying to help, and that if they had had better training, they might have been able to handle it differently. She just stared out and didn't answer them. What could she say? Nothing she could say would change what had happened. She brought her knees to her chest, wrapped her arms around them, leaned her head until her forehead was resting on them, and fought the tears that threatened to fall. She felt her friends' distress at not being able to find the words to give her the comfort they so desperately wanted to be able to give. She tried to tell them not to worry, that she would be all right, but the lie stuck in her throat. She wasn't sure she would ever be all right. She had made many mistakes but never one that had affected someone else in such a way. After several more moments of silence, her friends realized that she needed some time to herself. They started walking slowly towards the bungalow. She felt them stop several times and glance back her way. She wished she could give them some words of encouragement, but everything that came to mind just sounded so hollow to her. She felt the tree lean over her and felt a leafy branch gently caress her back as if soothing a child. She knew that was Vanna's last attempt at comfort, but she couldn't let go of her anger and angst.

The splashing of water drew her attention; she looked up to watch the antics of the mermaids and water nymphs. She was not sure how long she sat there staring at the mermaids who were splashing in the water as if a member of the Alpha group had not just been taken by the creatures they all feared. Over on the other side of the bank, she also saw a satyr chasing after a water nymph. She wondered how they couldn't feel the emptiness that you would feel at the loss of their missing comrade. She sighed a heavy sigh then leaned her head back against the tree, whose limbs had now returned to their proper place, and closed her eyes.

She didn't open them until she could feel the chill as a shadow blocked out the sun. She opened her eyes and saw that Raphael had joined her but rather than looking at her, he, too, was watching the activity around the lake. *Here we go.* Telara waited for the condemnation that she knew she well deserved. However, she was just not sure if she could handle it right now.

"So, is this how the youth of today handle complications that befall them?" he mused, watching with interest the satyr and nymph.

"Complications? Try catastrophe," Telara grunted. "That might sum it up better. A catastrophe of my own making." Raphael made it sound as if she had just left the fridge open all night rather than cost a friend his life.

"Really? It was all of your own making?" Raphael asked, still watching the two running awfully close to the water.

"I was the one who told Cole to join the handles so we could combine our powers to make the crystals burn brighter. Didn't bother to think that along with the minions, it would also blind our people, making them unable to defend themselves against the enemy," Telara said. "And now, thanks to my bright idea, the only one of the Alpha group that showed us any bit of kindness is gone, and his fate is as uncertain as the weather."

"Sanctuary's weather is always certain," Raphael said. "It is the inhabitants that reside here that are the uncertain ones."

She grimaced at that comment. "You know what I meant,"

she said. "And why are you not yelling at me telling me I screwed up?" she asked him.

"Is that what you want me to do?" he asked her.

"No, but that is what I expected you to do," she replied.

"Why?"

"Because even with all the training we received, I still screwed up," she explained.

"So you were the only one who was holding the crystal that blinded everyone?"

"Well, no, but Cole wouldn't have done it if I hadn't told him to."

"Really? And you were the one who said that you were no leader," he mused.

"That is not being a leader," Telara started to say then stopped as she realized he was right. She never had the ambition to lead, but it did seem that was exactly what she had done. She went quiet upon this revelation not sure what to say.

"Should you not warn Iago not to be so close to the water's edge?" Raphael said, gesturing towards the Satyr. "Any minute now, Siese will disappear into the water, and he might hurt himself falling in after her."

Telara frowned, looking over at the Satyr who howled with excitement as it seemed he was about ready to capture the elusive nymph.

"He has been doing this on an almost daily basis," she said, not understanding why Raphael would expect her to warn the Satyr. "He knows what to expect. The nymph lets him believe that he will catch her then, at the last minute, she will disappear in the water, and he usually ends up all wet. He has done it many times and knows what could happen chasing the nymph."

"Just like Gage knew what could happen going into battle as he had done many times before."

Telara pursed her lips as she realized that she had said exactly what he wanted her to say. But Raphael was not done with his points.

"Just like Pam knew what could happen taking in fighters who were not trained as properly as they should have been."

Still, Telara did not answer him but instead looked down at her hands.

"Just like Lucius should have known that you were not as informed as you should have been to take on such a task."

At Lucius' name, Telara's head jerked up, and she remembered how she and her friends had decided that after the battle they were going to find him and finally get the answers they needed. She stood up, brushed off the grass from her jeans, and looked at Raphael, who was finally looking at her. She began to see Raphael in a new light. He was still the overbearing drill inspector that hounded their every move in the training field, but he was also someone that actually cared about their wellbeing. That was just how he showed he cared.

She smiled at him and told him, "Thank you."

He just smiled at her and then took off back towards the fields. She turned and looked at the place that they had come to call home in the past few weeks, where they had started to discover their powers and found the confidence to use them. It was time to find the confidence to be able to be part of the whole Sanctuary. It was time for answers. With that thought giving her strength she never knew she possessed, she walked with a very determined pace into the Sanctuary and found her friends sitting in the common room.

Her friends looked up at her as she entered and saw the look on her face. They smiled at her, feeling as if they had their friend back. She could feel the relief in the room and smiled at them. Vanna came over and wrapped her arms around her, giving her a brief hug.

"So, what now commander?" she asked grinning cheekily.

"Now we get answers," Telara said, and the others nodded in agreement.

"About damn time," Cole said and put his arm around Telara. "This is the girl we have always followed and the one we will always follow. She is the one who managed to keep two boys from getting suspended for making a cherry bomb and then blowing over the football goal post."

"Yeah, figures the only time you two would take notes, and it gets you guys in trouble," Tia said giving him and Chad mock glares. "If Telara hadn't been there to get her brother to replace the goal post before Monday morning, you would have been suspended."

"If I remember correctly, you guys were told one more strike that year, and you were done," I.Q. said, grinning at the memory with the rest of them. They had been through so much together, and that was just the reminder that Telara needed.

Telara felt herself blush at their words. She never thought of herself as a leader but now she understood that she always had been. *It was time for this leader to lead her friends in the right direction.* They nodded in silent agreement.

"Well, right now there is only one person who can give us all the answers we seek. We're not leaving this place nor are we going to do another training session without answers," she said and closed her eyes.

She finally knew what she had to do and how to do it. With her mind, she searched through the building until she found the thoughts of the one whom she sought. Lucius was standing in a room with a desk that could only be his office. When she found him, he seemed to look right at her and, rather than seem upset at her intrusion, he smiled as if he was proud. She didn't dwell on this discovery; instead, she followed the trail that would lead them to him.

They found Lucius' office not far from the Static Room. As they approached the door, they stopped and stared as if dumbfounded. There, in front of them, was an oak door with a satin chrome knob handle. Telara stared at Tia then back to the door, not sure how to proceed. There was no crystal anywhere around the doorway. As a matter of fact, this doorway looked as normal as any door in the houses back home. Yet, here it looked completely out of place.

"That old dog," said Cole.

They turned to look at Cole.

"He is the black sheep of Sanctuary."

They started to laugh at that thought.

Telara grasped the knob and turned it only to find another surprise. There sat Lucius behind a rather plain oak desk; well, not plain compared to desks in the outside world, but to Sanctuary standards plain. His chair was of the same wood and leatherback. There were also oak bookshelves around the room with pictures and books lining them. The only other place here that had wooden furniture of any type was their hideaway. Everywhere else it was stone, glass, and crystal or a combination of them all. Telara was looking at the pictures that were situated on the bookshelves while the others eyed Lucius still seated behind his desk.

"Well, I am glad to see that you have started to feel more comfortable with your powers," Lucius said, pulling Telara away from the pictures and the questions that clouded her mind. She now had more questions than when she first entered, but she knew that the most recent ones were not as important as the original ones. So that is what she stuck with.

"We are done with the half-truths and the very little information that we have been given," Telara started out with a bit of aggression in her voice that at once she felt uncomfortable with. But when Lucius raised his eyebrows at her, she continued. "I don't mean any disrespect but my…" Telara stopped herself remembering her conversation with Raphael and amended her statement. "OUR failure today has put us all on edge."

She felt the others send their support to her and their approval in her amended wording. After all, they were supposed to be in this together.

"We need to know exactly why we are here and what is expected of us. We need enough information so that the next time you decide to send us into battle with creatures we have never seen, or with weapons that we don't know how to use, we will be able to better defend not only ourselves but others. Our mistakes are our own, but our mistakes are not entirely of our own making," she said and nervously waited for Lucius' response to her words.

She expected him to reprimand her for her audacity, so she was mildly surprised when he just smiled. He never seemed to do what was expected, so the surprise was not that great.

"Very well said," he said.

He stood up and walked over to the other side of the room to the huge window they hadn't noticed when they first walked into the room. They were astonished to see that just beyond the window was the Static Room. Had he been watching them the whole time they thought he had just left them to fumble on their own?

"Yes, I have been watching your progress with your

powers and have been very impressed with your progress, especially with as little training as you have received. I wasn't sure how well you would do." He turned back to them and, to their astonishment, said, "After all, you are the only Guardians to have received training at such a late stage in life."

12

"GUARDIANS?" Telara asked. "Pam has called us that a few times."

"Yes," Lucius nodded. "That is what you seven are."

"What does it mean?" Vanna crossed her legs on the ottoman on which she was sitting.

"It means a lot of things, but mostly it means you are to be the saviors, or Guardians as you will, of Sanctuary."

Telara frowned at Lucius. "We are to be the Saviors of Sanctuary? I thought we were just here to learn how to use our powers to defend ourselves from the Shadow creatures?"

Lucius took a deep breath and spoke with a very grave tone of voice, causing them to go very quiet. "While I have told you no lies, I have not been completely truthful with you." He stood up and walked over to the big window. "The role of Sanctuary is as I told you; we teach the descendants and train them to fight the Shadow creatures you have all seen. We provide a home and security to the mythical creatures that may not be as abundant as during ancient Greek times, but we keep the ones who still live alive. That is, in essence, the role of Sanctuary, but the role of a Guardian is more."

Lucius walked back over to his desk and looked at a vase that had etchings of people and animals all around. He looked as if he was trying to put his thoughts into words. He looked like he was afraid to say something wrong and scare them off.

"We haven't left yet," Telara pointed out, causing Lucius to whip his head around to stare at her in shock. "I can't read your thoughts if that is what you are thinking, but you had a very intense look on your face, like you were trying to figure out what to say without scaring us off."

Lucius gave a short chuckle. "Yeah, I guess I was." He sat down behind his desk and linked his fingers together before speaking. "To understand what your role is as Guardians, I will need to give you the history of Sanctuary."

"The Sanctuary has been around since the times of ancient Greek Gods." Lucius held up his hand as it seemed Telara was about to interrupt. "I understand that you already know that but to tell you all you need to know, I will need to tell you the story again."

Telara nodded her head in agreement and waited for him to continue. They didn't know what they were facing and if it meant hearing a few things twice to learn what they needed, Telara could handle that.

"What I am going to tell you here tonight you will find in no history book or in any mythology book in any library." Lucius absently rubbed his chin as if trying to figure out exactly where to start. "I guess the best place to start would be the beginning before Sanctuary was created." Lucius took a drink of the water from a cup that sat on his desk.

"Back before the Gods disappeared from the land, there

came a great evil. It was said this evil was as dark as a starless night, with no soul or heart."

"You are talking about the Shadows," Cole realized.

"I am talking about the origin of the Shadow Minions that you saw today," Lucius gently corrected him. "When the darkness first came to Greece, it not only had no name but also no corporal shape."

Chad was perched on the edge of his chair. "So….when did that change?"

"I will get to that," Lucius assured him. His solemn expression was a great contrast to the excitement on Chad's. That should have been a warning to them all about the story that was about to unfold. "Now, where was I? Oh yes. The darkness that had no name." Lucius leaned back in his chair, holding his fingertips together to form an arch. "This great evil was sweeping through the land, and any mortal unlucky enough to be caught in its path would lose all sense of being."

Tia wrinkled her nose at that last statement. "All sense of being?"

"I believe here in America there is a saying, "The lights are on, but no one is home.""

They gave a shudder at that thought.

"Wait a minute!" Cole protested. "The creatures today did nothing like that."

Lucius raised his eyebrows, effectively silencing Cole, who sat back in his chair.

"No, they did not," Lucius acknowledged. "But then again, the darkness I am talking about was no mere minion."

"With every empty shell the darkness left behind, it seemed to grow stronger. The people of Greece cried out for help, so the heroes of the land went hunting for this darkness to put an end to it once and for all."

"More lifeless shells," Vanna guessed glumly.

Lucius sadly shook his head. "Nothing. They were never seen nor heard from again. That became the fate of any hero, demi-god, or mortal that went in search of this Evil."

"The darkness seemed to thrive even more with these disappearances. As a matter of fact, it was during this time the first corporal dark figure was seen: a completely dark figure that was hunched over with long claws for hands and pointed teeth."

"The minions," Chad whispered.

Lucius nodded towards him. "Yes, we believe that those were the first sightings of the minions. These minions were not as powerful as the darkness that first came to Greece. Looking upon these creatures didn't cause anyone to lose sense of who they were. The only problem was that these minions were very strong, and their claws were very sharp. It seemed all they were interested in was capturing any creature or human they could come across and disappearing into the shadows with them. If the minion was able to pull a person into the shadows, it was too late. They would both disappear and, depending on who was taken, determined whether they would find a lifeless shell several days later along some road or nothing at all."

"Then the darkness discovered the mythical creatures that roamed Greece. It also discovered that their essence was equal to that of a demi-god; after all, most mythical creatures were children of Gods, and the magical blood they had was in abundance. The mythical creatures started disappearing almost to the point of extinction. With this new supply of essence, the darkness grew even more. With the minions, there came other Shadow creatures that were of an even greater threat. It was at this time that it was discovered that it was a being calling himself The Master that was behind all this."

"The Shadow Master?" Telara asked to which Lucius nodded.

"The Shadow Master had gained so much power he was finally able to create himself a corporal form. It was in this form that the Master led his army through Greece. With the mythicals on the verge of extinction, the heroes and demi-gods that still lived in Greece decided to make a place for them to live and be safe."

"Sanctuary," Telara smiled.

"Yes, that is when Sanctuary was created; it was to be a place of light when the world seemed to be swallowed by darkness. The people of Sanctuary called themselves the Arions. It is said that with some help by some of the Gods and Goddesses they made a safe haven for the mythical creatures of Greece. The heroes and demi-gods that hadn't been defeated by the Shadow Master became the fighters and defenders of Sanctuary. The great minds of Greece became Sanctuary's first scientists, engineers, and healers. Many earned positions of great authority."

"The army that the Shadow Master created was as heartless and soulless as its creator. It was unknown whether any had minds of their own or if they were mindless as well. It was known that they were ruthless and formidable as their numbers grew."

"Then came the day that everyone feared: the day the Shadow Army attacked Sanctuary. With all the magical blood that Sanctuary carried, the Shadow Master would end up with enough power that not even the Gods themselves would be able to defeat him. He would become unstoppable, and that the Gods refused to let happen. Therefore, the Gods and Goddesses, Olympian and Minor alike, joined with Sanctuary in this great battle. This battle waged for many days. It was said that the ground flowed with magical and Shadow blood alike. The land cried for the atrocities that were taking place in such a place of tranquility and peace. It is said that the Gods and Goddesses combined their powers with the blood of their descendants in an effort to destroy the Shadows. They created a blinding light so bright that no Shadow could escape. The light engulfed not only the whole of Sanctuary but also the surrounding mountains and land. When the light had dissipated, there was a feeling of great relief – the Great Evil that we know now as the Shadow Master and his armies were nowhere to be seen. But the losses in Sanctuary were great as well." Lucius bowed his head as if to say a silent prayer for the past losses.

"After this battle, the Gods disappeared from the land. Sanctuary was left on its own to protect the creatures and other Arions that were left."

"In the years that followed, Sanctuary thrived to become what you see today. The mythical creatures of Greece stayed here and made their homes and new lives free from the threat of persecution from humans that no longer believed in them or their beliefs. The Command Center became what you see today. There were many years of peace and tranquility experienced here."

"It was during this time that the crystals were discovered high up in the mountains where, to this day, you can see scars from that fateful battle. They were blood-red in color; hence, giving them the name of Blood Crystals. The scientists of that era were able to discover many uses for these Blood Crystals. They discovered the great power that resided in the crystals and used that to power the Command Center. The crystals also showed promise of other powers that were discovered throughout the years, and many that you have seen today."

"Now you know how and why Sanctuary came to be." Lucius smiled at them. "But that is not the end of the story. There is still the story of how the Guardians came to be and why you have been brought here."

"Over the years, the scientists of Sanctuary learned a great deal about the Blood Crystals. Not only were they good for powering the Command Center, but they discovered many other uses. It was discovered that mortals with magical blood were able to manipulate the crystals into implements of great use. The crystals were even capable of shielding Sanctuary from outside eyes."

"While the Arions were making headway with the crystals, unbeknownst to them, the Shadow Master was still very much alive. He had lost his corporal body and returned to the dark misty form that was first seen in Greece. Although his powers had been greatly weakened from his defeat, he was still able to plot his revenge against Sanctuary. He believed that if he was capable of defeating the Arions that lived here, he would be able to drain their magical essence and then the world would be his."

"A world of darkness," Vanna shuddered; she had always had a fear of dark places.

Lucius nodded to her assessment. "Even as weakened as he was, there was still essence for him to drain. The magical blood that lived before the Great Battle had thinned out considerably. It took much longer for him to amass his army than before and, without as much magical blood, they were not as powerful."

"The minions were once again sighted in Greece. The Sanctuary found itself fighting the Shadows yet again and, this time, there was no godly intervention. That was when it was discovered that the crystals, when in the hands of certain people, were able to create a weapon of light to battle the Shadows."

"With the Sanctuary using these new weapons to defeat the minions, the Shadow Master unveiled his most powerful and destructive creation yet: the Magine. The Magine was almost as powerful as the Shadow Master; it was definitely more powerful than any other Shadow creature the Master had created. Sanctuary lost many fighters and defenders to the Magine that fateful year. Their crystal weapons, while very powerful against minions and others in the Shadow Army, were about as effective as a knife in a gunfight when it came to the Magine." Lucius took a deep breath before continuing. "Everyone was beginning to believe that the Shadow Master would finally win and that there was no stopping him."

"But then the Magine was defeated by seven Arions that were said to be able to harness their powers without the aid of the crystals."

"The first Guardians?" Telara had tried to keep her thoughts to herself, but the question seemed to slip out before she could stop herself.

Lucius shook his head slowly. "No, they didn't carry the title of the Guardians, nor were they ever referred to as such. You see, the prophecy of the Guardians had not yet been spoken. They were just seven Arions that had banded together to defeat the Magine and save their home. Whether or not they had the help of the crystals or not has never been determined."

"So what? These seven defeat the Magine and save the Sanctuary and no one gives them recognition for being able to do such a feat?" I.Q. sounded very disgruntled at this thought. "You would think people would be very thankful for this."

Lucius held up his hand. "Don't get me wrong. The people of Sanctuary were very thankful, but the reason there is nothing more regarding these seven heroes was that after the battle, they never returned to Sanctuary."

"Why wouldn't they return to Sanctuary?" Cole asked.

"It was believed that they had perished in the battle."

"So how did the Guardians come into play if they weren't recognized as Guardians?" The knot in Telara's stomach seemed to grow with each passing moment.

"After the first battle with the Magine, there was a prophecy regarding the return of the new Magine."

"New Magine?" Cole sounded as worried as all of them felt.

"For all magical essence that would be lost in the world, a new Magine would be created. But the people had nothing to fear – for every Magine created from the darkness, there would be seven Guardians born of light to defeat this new evil."

"But we aren't the first Guardians." Telara chewed on her lip, trying not to show how freaked she was.

"No, you are the seventh set of Guardians as a matter of fact," Lucius said.

"Seventh set of Seven Guardians," I.Q. murmured almost to himself. Telara glanced over at him, but he was not looking at anyone in the room; he was looking out the great window very much deep in thought.

"Correct."

"But how did you know that we were the Guardians?" Telara protested. "I mean, yeah, we now know that we have these powers, but we didn't know that before we came here."

"You never had anything happen that was out of the ordinary and that other people may have perceived as being a peculiarity?" Lucius raised his eyebrows in question.

Telara conceded his point but still protested. "But how did you know that we were the Guardians?"

Lucius pointed to one of two dragon figurines that resided in the tallest bookshelf in the room. The dragon's tail wrapped around to create a base. The dragon seemed to be staring into the crystal that levitated between its claws. The black onyx dragon's crystal had a smoky mist swirling erratically around. The white marble dragon's crystal, on the other hand, had not only a white mist swirling in it but, as they looked closer, they also saw flashing images.

In one scene, they saw the hallway from the school where their lockers were located. They saw the altercation they had had with Raven and her boyfriend Bruce. They saw Bruce open his locker and all the contents of his locker sliding onto Bruce and landing on the floor. The next scene showed one of Bruce's lackeys, Jeff, shoving Chance aside to get a drink out of the water fountain. Then they saw a soaked Jeff glaring at Chance calling him jinxed. The nickname they had been branded with many times.

"The white crystal informs me that the Guardians are born."

"What about the black dragon crystal?" Telara was afraid of the answer; afraid she already knew it.

"When that glows, it means the Magine has risen and within the year will come to full power."

"Has it glowed yet?" You could hear the shiver in Tia's voice.

"No." They let out the breath they did not realize they were holding. "In the past, the Guardians have all reached their 18th year before the black dragon has awakened."

"Never before?" Cole cracked his knuckles; his face was a bit paler than before.

"It seems with every coming of the Guardians, it takes the Shadow Master longer to regenerate his new Magine. The supply of magical blood grows thinner as the years wear," Lucius tried to assure them.

"So the white dragon woke up telling you that we were born; yet, we never heard of any of this until now?" Telara was not sure whether she was thankful or upset over this news.

"In the past, when the white dragon had woken and we were finally led to the Guardians, we would find them in orphanages, abandoned by their parents for whatever reason." They looked at each other thinking that they were very lucky to have the parents they had. "We would then take guardianship of them and bring them here to learn of their heritage." The severity of all they were learning was apparent as there was no crack from Chad or Cole regarding Lucius being a guardian of the Guardians.

"When you were discovered with your parents, we had to take a different approach. But I promise you that you have been watched over since your discovery."

They looked at each other as each thought about all the times they would see figures hiding behind buildings or of having the feeling of being followed only to turn around and find no one there.

"Yes, that was us." As if he had read their minds Lucius answered their unspoken questions.

"Why did you never show yourselves?" Vanna asked.

Lucius smiled at her. "Every set of Guardians were brought here at such a young age and taught how to fight and use their powers. They never experienced what it was like to have a normal life outside of Sanctuary except for that in the orphanage, which you can imagine wasn't the best." They nodded in agreement. "It was decided that we would watch out for you until your powers were so apparent that there was no other course but to bring you here, or if it was too close to the time of the awakening of the Magine."

"So all the weird stuff that has been happening to us has been because our powers were growing?" I.Q. asked.

"Yes," Lucius nodded with a sad smile. "We couldn't afford for you to be in the dark anymore; your life as carefree teenagers had to come to an end."

"So, you came up with Camp Sanctuary and a rigged contest that we would, of course, win." Telara had no accusation in her voice.

Lucius nodded to her. "So now you know. You are the seven Guardians in the prophecy that are granted the power to take down the Magine."

"But how do we defeat the Magine?" Telara asked. "We don't even know what to do," she protested, sounding like Pam before their battle.

Lucius gave her a sad smile that spoke volumes. "You need to practice your powers, learn all you can from them. The crystals will help you if you let them."

"That is all?" Tia sounded perturbed as all of them felt. They expected more of an answer.

"Yes, that is all. Only when you learn your powers and all that they pertain to will you learn the knowledge of how to defeat the Magine."

"How long do we have?" I.Q. was watching the black dragon as if he expected it to come alive and try to devour them right where they sat.

Lucius looked over at the still dragon. "It is different with every set of Guardians due to the lack of magical blood the Shadow Master requires." Lucius looked at them with eyes filled with remorse. Telara had the feeling if he could save them from this fate he would.

"So we have a possibility of over 2 or 3 years?" Telara was also watching the dragon with great trepidation. She looked over at Lucius feeling the tears and fighting hard to hold them back and not show the fear she felt. "What if we were to just walk away?" She hated herself for asking, but she needed to know. "Let some other Guardians that can actually work their powers take on the Magine."

Lucius didn't reprimand her for being a coward. If anything, his solemn expression that he had had during their entire exchange turned to one of great sympathy, so much that all of them felt their stomachs tighten before he answered. "I'm afraid that is not possible. You see, there is only one set of Guardians for every Magine created. If the Magine comes to full power before you are able to defeat it, you will be the first the Magine will seek out. It will also destroy anyone that is in its path: innocent bystanders, your loved ones, even those you don't care for."

There were several minutes of silence as Lucius' words sank in. Telara stood up and, with legs that felt more like rubber, she walked over to stare out the window. The tranquil view of their room spread out before her.

"So we have no choice but to fulfill our destiny as the Guardians or we chance losing all that we hold dear," she stated more than asked.

Lucius nodded. "I'm afraid so."

Telara looked at her friends who were still seated with different expressions running across their faces. Tia was playing with her snake necklace and taking great pains not to look at the statues. Chance and Chad wore identical expressions of dread, which for these two identical twins didn't happen often. I.Q. seemed deep in thought staring at the wall behind where Lucius sat. Cole seemed unable to take his eyes off either dragon statue. Vanna had her arms wrapped tightly around her knees.

Telara looked back into their room, refusing to ask the one question that was on all of their minds. She was afraid if she heard the answer, she would lose what little courage she had.

Would they survive the battle?

13

———

Telara left the bungalow before her friends woke up; she had something she had to do, and she needed to do it alone. She walked into the Command Center with a very determined stride. Nothing was going to stop her from her mission; she had thought about this all night and right before morning had come to a conclusion. It was time to end this "learn what they needed to," and there was only one person who could help.

She found the person she was looking for sitting at her usual table with the rest of the Alpha Team, minus Gage, eating their breakfast. How odd not to see Gage's curly mop of brown hair sitting next to Pam and her signature ponytail. Pam looked up to see who had garnered the attention of the table but when she saw who it was, her lips pursed in irritation.

"We still have several hours before we need to deal with your presence," Pam said, turning back to her eggs and bacon.

"Tough," Telara said. "I have something to say, and I'm not leaving before I have my say."

"Then by all means," Pam said, pushing her plate back.

"My appetite is ruined now anyway."

Telara was surprised there was no jab about her being at fault for Gage's disappearance but chose not to dwell on that. She needed to say what was on her mind before she lost the nerve.

"I messed up, and I know it," Telara started, causing Pam to give a snort while the rest of the table shifted uncomfortably. "I got overconfident and rather than trying to work as a team I took it upon myself to take on creatures that I knew nothing about with a weapon that I was not familiar with." Several people at the table looked away, but Pam kept eye contact with her as she continued. "My decision cost everyone not only a good fighter but also a good friend. I would like to try to rectify the mistake that was made due to my inadequacies on the battlefield. For that, I need help. I need the best, and that, I have been told, is you."

Pam glanced away from Telara and looked with a sorrowful look in her eyes at the empty chair where Gage had always sat. There was something else in her eyes that Telara could not place, almost as if she felt a bit guilty herself, maybe for the fact that she should have started their training sooner than it was. Telara wasn't sure but right now she had a mission from which she wouldn't be deterred. Before this day was out, she needed Pam on her side, and Lucius had warned them not to let Pam know that they knew her story. Thus, Telara had to use what she could even knowing that Pam wanted to humiliate her; she was willing to accept that if it would get her the help needed.

"None of us could work the crystals worth a damn; we probably shouldn't have been out there as poorly prepared as we were. But since we are the Guardians and have this task ahead of us, we need to know what we're doing with in all aspects. I am asking for your help in teaching us how to use the crystals." Then, Telara surprised not only the table but herself by kneeling down on her knees in front of Pam. "No...I'm begging you to help us."

Pam stared at her as if she couldn't believe that she was actually down on her knees in the cafeteria begging for her help. Pam actually looked highly uncomfortable at that. Pam licked her lips.

"Maybe you weren't the only ones at fault," she admitted a bit slowly then turned to her team and told them to gather in the Alpha training room. A few smiled at her then gave nervous smiles to Telara and hurried away. Then she turned to Telara. "Can you have the others meet in the entry hall and then I will take you to our training room?"

Telara nodded, and they both walked side-by-side to meet the others who answered Telara's call as soon as they heard. At first, they were upset by her disappearance without informing them what she planned to do but after a few loud arguments, they agreed that it was necessary. They told her they would meet by the fountain and were waiting for her and Pam when they arrived. They gave a few half-smiles, not really sure what to say or how to react with the new situation in which they found themselves.

"We all started on the wrong foot, so I say we start all over," Vanna said, taking the lead and holding out her hand to Pam. "My name is Vanna; my friends call me Van, and I am what these guys call the Mother Hen of the group." Pam actually smiled at her and took her hand in a friendly shake. The others followed suit until it came Telara's turn.

Telara held out her hand and said, "The name is Telara; my friends call me Telly, and I am the unofficial leader of this motley crew who needs your help."

Pam smiled at her, also grasping her hand. "Well, my name is Pam, and I am the leader of the Alpha faction here at the Command Center. Glad to meet all of you and hope we will become friends."

"You're not the only ones who had a fault in the mistakes of our last battle…" Pam started to say.

Vanna interrupted her and said, "The past is the past, let's concentrate on our future."

Pam nodded gratefully at her.

"Well then shall we start your training in earnest this time?" Pam asked with a slight bow and smile. The guys all grinned, and the girls just shook their heads.

"Lead the way, el Capitan," Cole said with a very poor accent causing the guys to chuckle and the girls, Pam included, to give a little giggle.

The room to which Pam took them was not the training room but, in fact, a long room with several tables against the wall on one side. The four tables had many different sizes and colors of crystals, except for the very last table. On that table, there were containers along the top that were divided by sections. Inside the containers there looked to be different shapes and sizes of leather pieces. On the other side of the table there were identical containers but with silver pieces instead. On the ground by the first table was a bin with several compartments with different symbols on the top.

"In the bin are the crystals that have already been through status checking by the Gamma faction. They are the ones who determine the properties of a crystal. For example, whether one is offensive, defensive, or productive." At their confused expressions, she went on to say, "Offense crystals are used for our fighters, defense by our healers, and productive mostly by our maintenance."

"Maintenance?" Chad asked. The others shushed him and told him to listen.

But rather than be annoyed, Pam just smiled and informed him, "Yes, we do have maintenance here. They take care of the actual building and use the crystals to do that."

Pam motioned towards the four tables; each table had crystal centerpieces of different sizes and shapes. They appeared to be part of the table itself. They each had round smooth bases but had jagged pieces that protruded from the top. The first table's centerpiece was clear in color, and there were a few of the leather pieces that were strewn around the table. Pam informed them that the centerpieces were called the Parent Crystals, as they were what gave the Crims their power.

"Here is the healers' table. This is where the healing Crims and memory Crims are made that you saw our healers use yesterday."

"You mean the white coats?" Cole asked and earned a frown from Pam.

"That is what we called them as we didn't know exactly what to call them," Vanna said a bit sheepishly, glaring at Cole for making her make the admission.

Pam laughed. "Well, they are the only ones you will see in white coats around here so if you do want to call them that be my guest. But I would be careful not to say that out loud, not many of the healers have a sense of humor." She pointed to the leather straps they saw on the table. "It is rumored that the leather was crafted from the hide of Greek hinds, but that is yet to be proven." Pam shook her head. "Whether that is true or not, I don't know; it is my opinion it is just plain leather and that story was just made up to make it more interesting." With that, she gave a shrug of her shoulders and moved on to the next table.

Telara heard Chad and Cole whispering about how cool it would be to see a hind, the only creature whose blood was rumored to be able to kill a god.

"What did you mean by Crims?" Tia interrupted looking at the healers' table.

"Oh…Crims are what the factions here at the Command Center call the finished crystals," Pam explained. "Sorry, I keep forgetting that you guys know next to nothing about Sanctuary." She gave them a sheepish smile that each of them waved off as her statement was nothing but the truth. "They used to just be called crystals and by many they still are. I think that we are the first Command Center to refer to them as such." This probably explained why Lucius never told them they were called Crims.

The next table had a similar crystal in the center although there were smaller crystal pieces imbedded in the table around this centerpiece. The smaller pieces seemed to act as prisms with multiple colors reflecting off them onto the centerpiece. She told them this was for the illusion crystals that were also used yesterday along with creating other Crims with other features. The Crims from these crystals could be used by everyone at the Command Center, which they were told was very useful to help them keep Sanctuary the secret it was.

"Can Lucius use the crystals?" Tia asked.

"The Caretaker?" Pam mused. "Not really sure there. I have never seen him use any crystals; the only crystal he has ever had anything to do with is the one around his neck. And none of us know exactly what that one does, nor has he ever told anyone to my knowledge."

The third table Pam explained was where all the Crims for maintenance and other various functions around the Command Center were formed.

"These Crims you see around the Command Center are used for maintenance, whether it is for opening doors, giving light, or other various functions. It is not something you should ever have to worry about." She gave them a wry smile. "Maintenance workers are the brown or blue shirts you see walking around the Command Center."

Then, she motioned them towards the door to their right. They followed her through to a room that was wider than the previous room but not altogether bigger. In the center of the room, there was a table that resembled one you would see in a conference room. Across the top were several Crims that resembled the crystal wands that Pam had given them in the beginning.

As soon as they had entered this room, Telara felt a slight buzzing in her head, one that, since she had discovered her powers, had not been as prominent.

"What's wrong?" Tia asked, feeling her tension and causing the others to look her way also. Being able to sense each other's feelings was good in some ways but irritating in others. Telara shook her head as she didn't know what was causing the buzzing, and they turned back to Pam as she continued.

"Now each of the Crims that you see here on this table is as unique as the person that wields it," Pam told them then took out her Crim. She grasped it by the metal handle and held it straight out. They watched as the crystal grew from both ends as she held the center. Then she flung her arm straight down as if causing the crystal to flow down to where the handle was at the top of the long crystal staff.

"The Crim reacts to the wielder and becomes an extension of the wielder. But that is not the case with all Crims; if I were to pick up one of the wands that you see on the table, it would not work for me any more than the ones that you used worked for you." Pam had a look of chagrin on her face as they came to realize exactly what she meant when she said they were not the only ones at fault for their mistakes. But they had all decided to forget the past and concentrate on the future and so they just nodded and waited for her to continue.

When no recriminations came her way after her discloser, she gave them all a thankful smile.

"Where are the parent crystals for these Crims?" I.Q. asked.

"Those would be located in the Gamma quarters," Pam informed them. "No one but a Gamma is allowed access to them. The Crims are created there and stored in their vault until they receive an order to bring them here."

"Are you ready to find your Crim?" she asked them. They eyed the table with the crystal wand-like Crims that were scattered across the top.

"Go ahead." She gestured towards the table, but they just stared at her unsure of what they were to do.

"What are we supposed to do?" Cole asked uncertainty. He was staring at the crystal Crims on the table with the same expression that you would give when looking at a snake and trying to guess whether or not it was poisonous. Telara could well understand the feeling. After the battle that had blown up in their faces, she was not anymore keen on trying to figure out how to use them. However, Telara also knew that if they were to be better able to take on the minions or even the generals they needed to learn the practice of the crystals.

Pam actually gave them a sympathetic smile. Even though they had acted as friends in the past hour, it was still weird to see her give them anything other than her patent sneer.

"You will be the only ones who know. For me, when I walked up to the table, I felt a pull to my Crim. I can't tell you what you'll experience and not because of you being Guardians rather than just warriors," she hastened to add, "But everyone seems to describe the pull very differently. Gage said his crystal Crim called to him. All I can tell you is to walk up to the table and pick up whichever you feel might compliment you. If you don't feel anything then it is not for you." With that said she walked to the other side of the room and leaned against the wall to give them their own space.

All the Crims looked identical; there was nothing really that would make them stand out. Cole went forward and grabbed one off the table, waving the wand back and forth as if he was trying to cast a spell with it, causing all of them to laugh at the serious expression he wore. Pam even chuckled over it. She and Telara both smiled at each other as if they were watching the antics of a small child. He did this with several more until one that he grabbed suddenly glowed a bright red and two handles formed that were held together by a fiery red crystal-like chain. He looked at the others in surprise.

"Nunchucks!" he said just staring at them before giving them a silly grin. He stepped back from the table as Vanna walked up to pick out her Crim.

Vanna grabbed several, although to the disappointment of Cole, she did not wave them around. It only took her a few times before her crystal Crim glowed green and formed a staff that almost resembled Pam's. The main difference was that the metal handle had etchings of leaves woven through. Chad followed and when he found his Crim, the crystal turned an icy blue and formed into an ice sword. Luckily, when he waved the wand, no one was close to him. After that, everyone stood to the other side of the table so that when the Crim was discovered no one chanced losing an eye or anything else of value.

Telara, standing close to Pam by the door, felt the buzzing in her head seem to grow in intensity. She tried to focus on Chance and the Crim that would become his, but the buzzing was becoming a bit of a distraction.

Chance was a bit more cautious when testing out his. As with the others, the crystal glowed a light blue. From the crystal, a chain formed with a watery ball at the end.

"Ball and chain?" Cole said snickering.

"Otherwise known as a flail," Pam told them.

"Flail?" Chance looked at her.

"Look it up," she suggested, trying to hide her smile and not doing a very good job of it.

Chance stepped away from the table as I.Q. walked up. The first crystal Crim that he grabbed lit up with electricity that flowed through the crystal as it grew from both ends then curved until it resembled a bow, a very elegant looking one at that. As they watched, they could see a thin line of electricity stream from one end of the crystal to the other end until they could see the drawstring of the bow.

"All I am missing is arrows," I.Q. said, and he pulled the drawstring back as if to imitate firing off an arrow. When he let go, you could see the electrical bolt that flew from the bow into the wall right next to Cole's head. Cole jumped higher than he had during any of Raphael's exercises, and they stared at the scorch mark there in the wall that could have been Cole's head. For several minutes, they stared unable to speak.

I.Q. looked at Cole and stuttered, "S-s-sorry, Cole. I'm so sorry." His face was as pale as the white walls that surrounded the room.

Cole stared at him for another second before gasping out, "Dude! That was awesome!" He was grinning from ear-to-ear while I.Q. looked as if he was going to puke. "Man, why couldn't I get a bow?"

He looked back at the scorch mark that could have been his head and laughed. The others started to laugh with him. Leave it to Cole to be more impressed with the bow than the fact that he almost bit the dust. I.Q. was shaken after this experience, and they watched as his bow went back to its original shape. He sat down on the nearest chair and watched as Tia walked up to the table next.

Like I.Q., the first Crim she grabbed started to form her weapon of choice. They watched as the crystal grew in length until she was holding a crystal whip that seemed to swirl around her. They could feel the wind blowing gently from the whip and, with a swish of the whip, a blast of air blew gently around the room.

Telara looked at the table, knowing they were waiting for her. With a deep breath, she walked up to see if she could discover hers as quickly. As she walked closer to the table, the buzzing that she had been hearing seemed to fade. She felt a temporary relief that she could concentrate on the task in front of her. She had picked up each crystal wand that was left on the table, yet she felt nothing. On the last one, she even decided to wave it around as Cole had done but neither felt nor saw anything. She growled in frustration, flinging the wand back on the table causing it to knock several wands onto the floor. Pam chuckled while bending down to pick up the strays.

"I will have a note sent to Claw to let him know we are in need of some more crystals," Pam said then motioned for them to follow her out the door.

As they got closer to the door, the buzzing in Telara's head seemed to get louder until she had to lean against the table that was situated right by the door. It seemed harder to keep her balance with all the buzzing in her head.

"What is that?" Chance asked pointing to a swirling mass of what resembled a liquid version of the crystals with liquid metal that was floating in midair.

There were metal rods that were about six inches apart surrounding the swirling mass that was no bigger than his fist and as they watched, it was changing forms. It would create a circle that reminded Telara and Tia of bracelets they had worn when they were children. Then it split and twisted around as if it was imitating a small gardener snake. Telara was reminded of the shapes that danced around her ceiling at night. As she stared at the ever-changing mass, she felt something pulling her arm towards it. It was as if an invisible hand had reached out, grabbed her by the elbow, and was slowly pulling her hand forward. The buzzing had become so great that all she could feel was the invisible pull. She couldn't hear Pam yelling at her, telling her not to touch the liquid crystal. Before Pam or the others were able to pull back her hand, she passed the metal rods, and they watched as the liquid crystal changed to form a small rope that looped around Telara's wrist until it had formed into the bracelet yet again. Telara looked down at her wrist and realized that the buzzing was no longer there. She looked back at the others and saw Pam giving her a frightened look.

"What?" she asked.

"That should have taken your hand completely off," Pam said, staring at the bracelet with a touch of fear in her eyes.

"It didn't," Telara shrugged, feeling a bit more herself without the buzzing. "So you said something about training?" She smiled at Pam who slowly nodded her head then walked out the door ahead of them.

14

"Watch out!" Vanna yelled at Cole who was too busy trying to work his nunchucks to notice the dummy that flew his way. I.Q. flew an electrical arrow to knock the dummy off course, which caused the dummy to explode into many pieces that peppered a dumbstruck Cole.

"Hey!" he yelled at I.Q. "What did you do that for?" he asked, brushing off the bits of wood and burnt straw that was sticking to his clothes and hair.

"Next time, I will let the dummy hit ya," I.Q. told him. "Maybe it will knock some sense into you." Cole just glared and went back to trying to take down the moving dummy with his fiery nunchucks.

Telara smiled watching their antics. They were all getting really good with their Crims, and they had only been there for an hour or so. If only they could work their powers as well as they seemed to work these Crims. The dummies now moved and would actually try to take them out, and their job was to incapacitate them. Vanna was able to make her staff extend out and in on command. She learned fairly quickly, though, that she needed to pay attention more to the dummies than her pretty staff. The dummies would attack while she was staring at the intricate patterns that would appear around her staff as the crystals would extend, knocking her to the ground. She managed to sweep the staff at one dummy, knocking its legs out from underneath it.

After a few bruises, Chance learned not to get too excited with his flail while he was swinging it around. Once, he swung it around his head to take out a dummy that was about to grab Tia from behind and ended up with a goose egg, causing the Alpha faction to chuckle. One of the girls took pity on him. Her name was Stella. She had brown hair that was always pulled back in a ponytail although not as tight as Pam's. She showed Chance how to use the flail so as to not hit himself in the head with it. Pam leaned over to tell Telara that Stella was their very own weapon expert; there wasn't a weapon with which Stella had not trained with. Her own Crim, as a matter of fact, would change its shape to conform to what Stella was in the mood for. The only weapon she didn't care for was the bows.

While Stella was busy helping out Chance, his brother was making fast work of any dummy that came close to him with his ice sword. Not only was he cutting them right in half but where the crystal touched, you would see icy film appear. Tia was using her whip without any of the help that the others seemed to need, probably due to her rodeo days. Telara smiled remembering all the times Tia would take down the calf with ease as if she and the rope were one, kind of like now. She could use the whip to pull a dummy away from one of them or to create a gust of wind to knock it down. It seemed they were all taking very well to their crystal weapons. All except her. Telara looked down at the bracelet that circled her wrist. The liquids of crystal and metal both were constantly moving; yet, it felt still to her.

"Hey, don't feel bad," Pam told her after watching her for several minutes. "There is not one of us here that would know how to use the rotary. Even Claw has not been able to figure out its secrets."

"What do you mean?"

"Apparently, the rotary just showed up one day in that room on that table with those metal rods surrounding it as it hung in midair. It was unable to be moved and after one of the Gamma members lost their hand trying to figure it out, it was deemed off-limits." Pam shrugged.

"Is that how Claw got his name?"

"Wha…? Oh no, it wasn't Claw who lost his hand," Pam chuckled. "If you happen to meet Claw, I would keep any questions regarding his name to yourself."

Telara shrugged. "I'm not out to offend anyone."

Pam licked her lips. "I'm not sure if it is even possible to offend him." Telara gave her a curious look. "Claw is a bit… crass I guess would be the best description. Eccentric is another one, but I definitely wouldn't call him that to his face; he is a bit touchy on that. He is of Scottish descent with the hair and temper to match. He can be abrasive, argumentative, and downright instigative, but he is also the best at what he does."

Pam grimaced and turned back to the others who were enjoying themselves and exhausting the supply of moving dummies. "I wouldn't worry about it much; it attached itself to you, so that means it was meant for you. When you have need of it, I am betting that it will show its true powers to ya."

"Yeah, well I would rather go into battle with a bit more confidence in my ability to work it," Telara said with a bite.

Pam chuckled. "Patience, my young apprentice." That earned her a glare from Telara who told her that she was a bit on the tall side for that old movie phrase to work.

"Yeah, and I also think I'm not green enough," Telara replied.

"Did someone mention lunch?" Chad strolled up to them which caused them to laugh.

"Lunchtime sounds good," Pam agreed.

This time around, they sat with Pam and her group at her table ignoring all the incredulous looks that were thrown their way. Pam had told them that there was a table set up just for the Guardians at the head of the room where they should have sat the first time. Telara and the others agreed that they didn't care to sit by themselves; they would rather sit with their new friends which caused the whole Alpha team to get tinges of pink around their cheeks. After lunch, they walked around Sanctuary with Pam and discovered more about the Command Center.

There were several different departments that took care of Sanctuary as a whole. The top of the list was the Leaders who decided what law was and what was not. Apparently, Lucius and Ira both reported directly to them.

"Of course with Lucius, you never know if he is humoring them or actually doing what they want him to do. Ira has complained of this many times, but it is still the same," Pam chuckled. However, when I.Q. asked her who the leaders were, she had to tell them that she didn't know. "The only ones who speak to them are Ira and Lucius."

After the leaders was the Defense Department, which was divided into factions that Ira commanded. Pam, as Alpha leader, was second-in-command.

"We are considered the Enforcers. Pretty much, we oversee

all the groups and make sure all is running as should be. We take on the major fights that take place outside Sanctuary where there are innocents in danger."

She went on to tell them about the second faction, the Beta group, who also took care of Exterior Defense. "We are supposed to work together to keep all innocents safe. Their leader is Carmen and if you thought I had an attitude when you first met me, you haven't seen anything yet. I have been told I am a pussy cat compared to her. She likes her position and will let no one damage it. Even her own faction is wary of getting on her bad side."

"Great!" Cole threw his hands up in the air. "We finally make nice with the witch of the west and now we find there is even a worse one in the witch of the east. Ouch!" He rubbed his arm where Tia had belted him. He gave Pam a sheepish look. "Sorry."

Pam just laughed. "No reason to be sorry; that was the image I was going for, so I am glad that I was able to achieve my goal. Just a fair warning: I did pass Witchcraft 101. Ever thought about a new image as a toad?"

Everyone got a good chuckle from that; well, all except for Cole.

"Anyways, on to the next faction. That would be Gamma group who are our weapon specialists. As I said before, they are the ones who create the weapons that are used here at Sanctuary."

"With a very unstable leader," Telara said cheekily.

Pam grimaced. "I really hope you never meet him."

Pam turned the corner that headed to the courtyard. "The Gamma group is comprised of ones who have descended from others who were able to create certain types of weapons. Ira and Claw don't get along because Claw always wants to make weapons other than the norm. Ira has told him many times to just stick to the procedure, which is to create the Crims that would conform to only a certain person."

"Other than the norm?" Telara questioned.

"It seems to me that they transform into different weapons as is," Cole said.

"Well....Claw apparently believed he could make weapons that would rival even the powers of the Guardians." Pam grinned at Telara's raised eyebrows. "Another one of the Gamma's specialties is to determine whether the crystals are high power, low power, or..." Pam paused as she glanced at the bracelet on Telara's wrist. "Unstable."

Telara gave a nervous look at her wrist. "This was determined unstable, and it is now on me?"

"No worries. The ones they call unstable are because they were unable to determine its origin or its use." Pam nodded to a platinum blonde white coat as they came upon the fountain. "I wouldn't worry about it if I were you."

"You're not me." Telara could not take her eyes off the bracelet.

Pam went on to explain that the next faction was the Delta group who were the monitors/trackers of the Command Center. "They are the ones you will see in the Command Room where we first met. They are on the highest row watching the monitors. If they are not there that is because they are tracking rouges."

"Rouges?" Chance asked.

"Sometimes, either mythicals or even Command workers go rouge and when that happens, they need to be found quickly. They also are the ones who report Shadow sightings and can pretty much tell you what to expect." Pam shrugged then quickly went on to tell them about the Theta group who were in charge of Patrol. "They patrol the grounds of Sanctuary. You usually won't really see them or the Omegas, who are considered our generalized peacekeepers."

"Generalized peacekeepers?" Telara frowned finally finding something to take her mind off her unstable bracelet.

"They take care of any minor disturbances from any of the mythicals around Sanctuary. You know, one of the Harlick brothers decided to pinch some ale from the Grendow sisters, and we had acorns and branches flying everywhere." Pam shrugged. "And that covers the defense, not that you will probably meet any of them. Now then, we have the Janitorial department that is mostly satyrs and…"

"Why?" Vanna queried.

"Because even a place as magical as this gets dirty." Pam shook her head as if that was a silly question.

"No, I mean why won't we meet any of them?" Vanna rephrased, and the others looked interested in the answer to this question.

Pam shrugged her shoulders. "No reason really; it was just never part of the itinerary of your training."

"Itinerary?" Tia looked at Telara who shrugged; she didn't know about any itinerary either.

"Last year, all leads were informed the Guardians would be coming to Sanctuary. We were told your fighting training would be overseen by Raphael while Alpha faction would take up crystal training." She gave them a grin. "When one of the other factions spoke up about their role, Ira informed them their role is to stay out of the way."

"Harsh!" Chad exclaimed.

Pam grimaced. "Yeah, that is pretty much the way it was taken, but Ira explained to me afterward that the Guardians were being brought here later in life than the previous ones."

They nodded. After all, that is what Lucius had already told them. "Well, Ira was pretty upset about this. He said it didn't give us much time to train you. He said he wasn't going to deal with any hero worship that would distract you from training."

"Hero worship?" Tia's eyes widened. They remembered Pam's vehement spiel the first day they had met.

"According to Sanctuary's history books, that was very common with every Guardian, which was fine back then. The Guardians had more time than you guys to train."

"Somehow, I don't think Ira needs to worry about that," Telara laughed but stopped suddenly as a thought occurred to her. "Did he forbid them to interact with us or pass a law saying as much?"

Pam frowned. "No."

"Well, then there is no reason we can't go introduce ourselves to them." Telara smiled.

"But meeting them will not benefit your training," Pam protested.

"Do we have to benefit from being introduced to possible new friends?" Vanna crossed her arms.

Pam laughed out loud. "You guys are definitely going to shake this place up." None of them really understood what she meant by that. "You want to meet the other factions then I will see what I can do."

With that, she gave them a wave and, to their astonishment, blew a surprised Raphael a kiss before disappearing around the corner. Raphael raised his eyebrows in question causing them to erupt in laughter.

15
———

TELARA STARED out at Mermaid Lake and at Brom and her friends who were playing a game of keep-away with one of the water nymphs. They kept throwing the seashell over her head until, with a spray of water, the nymph grasped the shell and disappeared under the water's surface. Brom was laughing with her friends as they were pelted with water from the nymph's dive. Brom stopped laughing and stared at them as if she had just noticed them. Telara was confused by this as they had sat on the shore many times watching Brom with her friends and sisters, and the mermaid had never paid them much attention.

"Wonder what has her giving us such curious looks?" Cole mused out loud.

"I think it has more to do with me being here than you guys," Pam chuckled behind them causing them to jump in surprise. "Hey!" Pam held up her hands and laughed. "You guys said you were interested in meeting more than just me and my crew."

"Sorry, we were just deep in thought and not paying much attention to our surroundings," Vanna explained.

Pam raised her eyebrows at that. "Shouldn't the Guardians always be on guard?"

"Why should we expect an attack here this deep in Sanctuary?" Telara lay back on the grass. "And why would she be surprised to see you here? I mean, after all, weren't you born here?"

"We have never had an attack this deep in Sanctuary that I have ever heard of but, then again, it has been a long time since the last appearance of the Guardians. I don't know myself what the Guardians should be expecting; you guys would know more than me." Telara gave a disgusted grunt at that which Pam ignored. She continued. "As to why Brom would be surprised to see me here, that is simple. No one other than the Caretaker or the Guardians has ever been allowed in this area of Sanctuary."

"Not even Ira?" Telara questioned her, thinking back to the first night she had ever dream walked.

"Not that I am aware of." Pam sat down next to her. "We have always been taught that our place is in the Command Center, and this was place was off-limits. I had to do some fancy footwork to sneak out here without anyone seeing."

"Well, that is silly," Vanna piped up. "What Guardians are not allowed visitors? That would be awful lonely for them."

"So who do you have in mind for this meet and greet?" Telara looked over at Pam who just shrugged.

"I guess that would be up to you guys. The Sanctuary is actually a pretty big place, and I am sure that you don't want to take another tour through the Command Center." They shook their heads at that causing Pam to chuckle. "You sure there are some parts that you haven't seen?" Pam held up her hands in mock surrender at their expressions. "Okay – Okay – Give! Well, I believe you met the fairies and honestly, it is a bit late to be calling on them. They go to bed pretty early and don't like to be woken up. The sprites are up all hours of the night, but I would rather not bother them and trust me, you don't want to either. Once you have entered their domain, they consider you fair game for life." Pam shuddered and held up her hands. "I won't even tell you any of the incidents, but you can trust me they are better left alone." Telara shook her head at the gleam of interest that showed in both Chad's and Chance's eyes. "There is not much in Fable Forest but sleeping nymphs and trees. Well, not all nymphs are sleeping but as with the fairies, we don't disturb them. Then there is the Centaur Village, but they get even crankier than the fairies at being disturbed."

"So, in other words, don't disturb anyone that is sleeping?" Vanna questioned.

Pam chuckled "Pretty much. Then you have Thetis village, and there is where most of the mythicals of Sanctuary work and live."

Telara stood up. "Let's have some fun."

Pam looked wary. "Exactly what do you have in mind?"

"I don't know about these guys, but I would love to see this village that we keep hearing in passing," Telara stated in the same upbeat tone as if they were talking about going to see a movie they have been dying to see.

Pam shrugged her shoulders and stood up. "Let's go."

As they walked, Cole muttered underneath his breath.

"And what happened, then? Well, in Whoville they say that the Grinch's small hairband grew three sizes that day, and her hair fell down her shoulders in glorious waves."

That was when they all realized that Pam's hair was indeed

hanging down, and there was a bit of a wave to her locks. Pam gave him a curious look, and Tia elbowed him shaking her head at Pam who just shrugged.

They followed Pam through the woods past the Elder Tree and along a very small path that, without Pam pointing it out, they would have never seen. When Cole said as much, Pam just smiled and told him that was the idea. As they walked, they could see several nymphs giggling and running through the woods.

So much for them sleeping. Telara grinned at Tia who replied back, *She did say most.* Telara shrugged and kept walking.

They watched as one nymph made a graceful leap over a fallen tree, reminding them of a gazelle running. Pam told her that was Gina, a tree nymph that had a very mischievous streak. She told them they needed to be careful around her or else they might find themselves permanently attached to a tree. She told them how Gina once fancied Gage. Gage, on the other hand, thought she was cute and nice, but he had no romantic interest in her. When Gina tried to get him to chase her through the woods once, Gage let her believe that he was following her and instead he went the other way and headed back to the Command Center.

"The following day, we went looking for him because he had missed practice. We found him; he was tied to the elder tree with several other trees blocking him in." Pam laughed at the memory. "It took us getting Lucius involved to get him out of that. Lucius had to explain to Gina that just because someone spurned her advances she couldn't take it upon herself to chain them to a tree."

"I will definitely be careful then," Cole said with his head high and a smile on his face.

"I don't think you will have anything to worry about," Pam

assured him ignoring his indignant look. "She has a thing for the quiet guys."

"Well, that leaves you two out," Chance said gesturing towards Cole and Chad. Their laughter stopped when they finally made it out of the trees and saw their destination.

"Welcome to Thetis," Pam announced. "This is where most of the mythical creatures of Sanctuary live."

She gestured around them at the houses and buildings. They looked as if they came out of a fairy tale story. There were all shapes and sizes; some looked to be made out of wood or straw, and one even looked too be made completely out of grass leaves and flowers. There were many that looked as if toddlers lived there, they were so small. They saw a few that were made out of stone with sculptures of different animals alongside the house. The roads were either dirt or cobblestone with old fashioned lamps lighting the way. Tia pointed up into the trees, and they saw homes that were built right into the trees themselves. Pam pointed down a road that went away from the town and told them that was where Raphael lived with the other centaurs.

Chance leaned against a tree trunk staring out over the village where they could see many creatures of all sorts walking through the streets. They saw three old women sitting in lawn chairs outside a house that was built into a tree. They watched as they seemed to be arguing over some ball of some sort.

"Ewwwww." Vanna gave a shudder. "Is that an eye?"

Pam gave a chuckle "That would be the Graeae sisters."

"What are you staring at?"

Telara turned around and saw Chance giving his brother an irritated look. Chad was staring up at the tree that Chance was leaning against with his mouth open, reminding Telara of one of those lawn decorations with different animals that were used to catch water.

"Better hope there is no rain or else you might drown."

They chuckled at Telara's statement, but Chad still stared until Pam realized what had caught his eye.

"Meet Talos, the guardian of Thetis," she told them, causing them to look up and realize that it was not a tree that Chance was leaning up against but a giant man.

Chance jumped back a few feet upon realizing what Pam had meant.

"A-a-a giant?" he asked with a quiver to his voice.

"No, an automaton; the one that used to protect Europa as a matter of fact," she told them as if every city had a giant automaton standing guard. "No worries; he will not come to life unless the town is threatened."

"Well, big dude, no worries from us; we are just here to have some fun," Chance told him, his voice still a bit shaky.

They laughed a bit nervously and moved quickly away from the statue. They followed Pam down a cobblestone path until they came to a wooden building with a sign outside that read: Czaar's Cantina.

"A bar?" Chad asked excitedly.

"Tavern," Pam supplied. "But yeah, I guess you could say bar although I wouldn't try for any alcoholic beverage. Silest has rules against serving minors, and her rules are always followed. Come on in and meet some of the townsfolk."

They walked through the door. Inside, they saw not only humans sitting and standing but also many creatures that they had only seen in books and read about in stories. Off to one side, they saw satyrs and two human guys standing around what resembled an air hockey table. The sides resembled bumper pads while the glass balls flying across the surface looked like very large marbles with flashing lights inside. One ball hit a bumper and disappeared causing the table to light up and the satyrs to high five each other. A nymph with leaves and twigs in her hair wrapped her arms around one of the satyrs and planted a kiss on his cheek. They saw some gnomes drinking from tankards in a corner staring around the room with their beady eyes and grumbling to one another. Behind the bar was a very gorgeous woman with bright red hair. Cole started to amble towards the bar but jumped back when they saw a green scaly tail from behind the woman grab a glass from behind her and set it down in front of her. They watched as she calmly filled the glass with some red liquid from the decanter.

"That would be our resident Dracaena," Pam told them then steered them over to a table where the rest of the Alpha group were sitting.

"Dracaenae?" I.Q. queried. "As in Echidna?"

"Actually, she is a direct descendant of Echidna; her name is Daphne," Pam told them. "But no worries; she is a lot nicer."

"And very good for me busssssinesssss."

They turned around and saw a woman slithering – that could be the only way to describe it – toward them. Her head and torso were that of a very beautiful woman, even more so than the bartender, but as you looked lower you saw that the rest of her body was that of a serpent.

"Guys meet Silest. She owns Czaar's Cantina," Pam said smiling at Silest.

"And who do we have here?" Silest asked in her very silky voice looking Chance over very curiously. "And are they taken?"

Pam was trying very hard not to laugh as Chance started to squirm under Silest's very intent gaze.

"Actually, Silest, I would like to introduce you to the Guardians – Chance – the one who has caught your eye, Chad – his twin brother if you can't tell, I.Q. – and yes his name matches his intellect, Cole – the Romeo of the bunch, Vanna – the quiet one of the bunch, Tia – the one refusing to sit down, and finally there is Telara – the leader of this motley crew." Pam smiled at Telara with raised brows and asked, "Did I get it right?"

Telara had to laugh at that. "Pretty much." She turned towards Silest "Nice to meet you." But Silest was staring at them as if they had suddenly grown several heads and were breathing fire. "What did we do wrong?"

"Nothing," Pam said glaring at Silest. "It has just been so long, many wondered if the Guardians were actually real or just a myth." Telara almost laughed at the thought that the creatures here thought they were just a myth.

"And my place is the first they vissssssited," Silest said with a gleam in her eye. "Wait until I write home about thissssss. Have whatever you would like; it isssss on the housssssse."

With that, she slithered away, leaving everyone– except for the Alpha group – very confused.

"Don't worry about it," Pam chuckled. "Actually, better get used to it. All I can tell you is what I have heard, considering you are the only Guardians I have ever actually met."

"Uhhh-kay," Telara said slowly. "How did she know this was the first place we visited?"

"Silest has her ways of finding out information that no one else knows." Pam shrugged.

Tia sat down next to Telara. "And no one wonders why?"

Pam gave a halfhearted chuckle. "More like no one can figure it out. Silest is definitely what you would call a character."

Cole cleared his throat. "So is this the reaction we are gonna get from everyone here?"

Pam took a drink of her juice before answering. "Probably; better get used to it. The stories that are told about past Guardians paint them as very anti-social." Pam chewed on her bottom lip as though she wanted to say something else but thought better of it. "I don't even know why they have their own table in the dining hall. From what we have been told, they don't dine there."

"Wait," Tia interrupted. "You mean past Guardians never interacted with any of the people here?"

Pam shrugged her shoulders. "I don't know of anyone who has met any Guardian personally. It has been too long since the last Guardians were around, so all anyone has to go off is stories of old. Those stories do not paint the Guardians in much of a social light. They are brought to the Sanctuary to learn their powers and the crystals, to prepare them to take on the Magine. I don't even know if any of the past Guardians participated in any small battles such as the one you guys did with us. Many here were beginning to believe that that is just what they were – stories. Actually, I think you are the only Guardians from America."

"So, in other words, a tradition of train, train, fight. Not much of a life." Tia grimaced.

Pam agreed. "But hey, you could always break tradition," Pam told her with a smile.

"Hey, we are good at breaking things," Chad said with a smirk.

"Got that one right," I.Q. said shaking his head.

Telara was sitting there looking around the room. She saw that there were many creatures and humans alike sharing a drink and just talking as if this was an everyday occurrence.

Of course to them, it probably is. Tia smiled at her thoughts but didn't say anything. They spent the better part of the next hour just talking and taking in the place.

Tia noticed a woman who was singing over in the far corner. Her voice was very melodic and enchanting. It was like nothing they had ever heard back home. Tia pointed her out to Telara, who looked over and had to give a second look before chuckling and shaking her head.

"What is it?" Pam asked her looking over to where they were staring. "Ahhh, meet Serdita, the Czaar's very own Siren."

They looked over this time at Serdita with her blonde hair that looked as if the long locks were blowing in a permanent wind; yet, there was no wind to be found. Her wings were folded together behind her. They couldn't see her legs nor her feet as a long shimmering pink gown covered them completely. She looked just like a very beautiful woman with wings that almost matched her beauty. They wanted to ask if her legs were human too, but figured that would be rude.

"Siren?" I.Q. glanced at Pam then back to Serdita. "You mean as in the ones who tempt men to their deaths?" Cole, Chad, and Chance gave visible shivers at hearing this.

Pam gave a laugh. "The very same. Although, you won't find this one trying to lure any man to his death. She just likes to sing with her Chenras."

"Chenras?" Tia looked over at Serdita to see if she could discover them.

"The silver balls you see on her hands that move between her fingers;" Pam pointed out. "They are called Chenras, and they are what are making the music you hear."

"The music is very different than any kind I have ever heard," Tia stated, this time staring at the silver Chenras that seemed to be moving with very little effort around Serdita's hands. At one point, they wove around her wrist before returning to climb up the thumb and finish the route around her hand.

"Well, the Chenra is a musical enchantment that supposedly can sound different to everyone who hears it." Pam shrugged. "But it seems here we all hear the same musical chimes."

"I don't know; it sounds a bit rock-n- roll to me," Chance grinned.

Pam shook her head. "Well, then maybe the legends are true, and you are hearing what sounds are pleasing to you. Most of us come in here to unwind, so the simple melody is what we need to hear."

"Where can you get one of these Chenras?" Tia was still staring at Serdita's hands with a longing expression on her face, causing the others to chuckle. Tia loved music, and any type of new musical instrument she always wanted to play.

"You can't." Tia looked over at Pam with questioning eyes. "The Chenras were not created from anything that I know of. As a matter of fact, no one knows what they are made of or if they are actually alive."

"How can no one know?" I.Q. asked, staring at the Chenras like he would a specimen under a microscope. I.Q. is one who hates not knowing how things work, which is what surprised Telara the most about him wanting to stay after their first week here.

"There are only two people who know anything about the Chenras," Pam said nodding towards Serdita. "Serdita and her sister Soliel."

Tia sat back disgruntled that she would never be able to own a Chenra. She glanced at Pam out of the corner of her eye.

"Do you think if I asked very nicely that Serdita would let me check out her Chenra?"

"I wouldn't," Pam advised looking very serious. "Those two sisters are very protective of the Chenras. I would just leave this one alone if I were you."

"So who is that?" Vanna changed the subject nodding over to the table where a blonde guy was sitting with several gnomes and what looked like another tree nymph with leaves in her hair. He had been glancing over towards their table with a very intense look.

"Gabe? That would be the leader of the Theta group. Pretty decent guy and not bad looking either," Pam said with a smile. Vanna smiled over at the guy but didn't get up and say hello.

"They are the ones in charge of patrol, right?" Telara was staring at the blonde when a redhead with a Command Center uniform approached him with a tablet in her hand.

"Yea-a-a," Pam said. "Exactly what are you thinking?"

Telara just smiled "I think it is time we introduced ourselves."

"Oh boy," Vanna said but rose with the others to walk towards the Theta leader.

Gabe looked up, and they saw his gray eyes widen as he realized who was approaching his table. The gnomes at the table just ignored them, but the tree nymph looked very intrigued. Telara held out her hand

"Hello! My name is Telara, and these are my friends: Tia, Vanna, Cole, Chad, Chance, and I.Q."

Gabe took her hand then smiled at Vanna who turned a bit pink. He turned back to Telara. "I know who you are; I don't think there are many people here who don't know the great Guardians."

This comment rankled Telara, but she bit her tongue. It

seemed that even though the Guardians were the saviors of Sanctuary, they didn't have a good reputation, or at least any type of rep Telara would find attractive.

"Some might not be too happy with your presence though."

Vanna frowned. "Why? What have we done?"

Gabe smiled at her and winked. "No worries, sweetness. You haven't done anything wrong, but there were many bets as to whether or not the Guardians were real. And now, after all these years, it's pay up time."

He chuckled, glancing at one of the surly gnomes who just harrumphed before plopping down out of his chair with a light thump and walking away. He was followed by his friends along with the tree nymph who reluctantly followed them to the corner table. Gabe looked back at them.

"So, now that you have chased off my companions, to what do I owe this great honor?"

Telara got the feeling this guy was definitely a smooth talker, but she felt no animosity from him, just great curiosity especially when those gray eyes of his caught Vanna peeking out from beneath her brown and copper locks of hair.

"No honor; just wanted to meet with you; we are, after all, on the same side."

Gabe's eyebrows rose. "Really? Well, this will definitely be something to put into my diary."

"You have a diary?" Chad asked looking at Gabe weirdly.

Gabe just ignored him and motioned for them to take a seat. They had to drag some chairs from other tables but eventually, they were all seated somewhat around the table. Gabe kept staring at Vanna who was going between looking at him under her lashes to flicking her beaded bracelet.

"So I hear your faction does all patrols around Sanctuary?"

Telara questioned to not only break the ice but also get Gabe's attention before Vanna melted on the spot.

"Yes, we do." Gabe gave Telara his attention with a smile. "Why? Would you like to maybe join us and see how the underdogs swing it?" He took a swig of his pop.

Telara was about to laugh. Then, before she could stop herself, she answered, "As a matter of fact, I think we would."

Gabe almost choked on his pop, but he recovered quickly with watery eyes to give Telara an incredulous look. "Did I hear you right? You would like to do a patrol with me and my faction?"

"Yes," Telara replied ignoring the others' look of surprise.

"Well then blue eyes," Gabe said rising from his seat and looking at his watch. "The Theta group will meet you tomorrow night after dinner by the Elder Tree."

With that said he waved to Silest and sauntered out the door.

16

———

"You son of a big-nosed Lorax!"

Cole put his hand over his mouth to try to stifle the chuckle, earning him a glare from Brie, Gabe's second-in-command. They were slouched over due to the low ceiling in the home of Tad and Shirk Harlick, the gnome brothers who lived in one of the treehouses outside of town. They had been strolling around Sanctuary with Gabe and his troop on their patrol when they got the word that there was a disturbance on the south side of town. Gabe groaned and informed them that at least 50% of the disturbance calls were due to the Harlick brothers who fought with the Grendow sisters.

Chez, a red-haired Romeo with freckles and also a member of the Theta group, chuckled and said, "I believe it has more to do with an infatuation rather than an irritation.

"I thought the Omegas were the generalized peacekeepers around Sanctuary?" Vanna asked Gabe as they walked the outskirts of Thetis.

Gabe chuckled and flicked her nose, earning him a glare from her. "That is what Command Center protocol tells us, but

Theta and Omega factions like to think outside the box. I told Tobias I would take this sector today."

"Wanting to have something to show the Guardians?" Cole smirked.

Gabe stopped and turned right around. "Let's get one thing straight: I don't need to show anybody anything; you guys are the ones who wanted to tag along."

Cole's smirk disappeared, and he actually looked contrite. Gabe continued as if that little altercation never happened. "Omega and Theta factions are the only factions that actually work together here at Sanctuary. We help with keeping the peace with the residents, and they have helped with our border patrol from time-to-time."

"So factions can actually work together?" Tia queried.

Gabe grunted. "Not all, girly." Tia wrinkled her nose at that moniker. At least it wasn't sweetness. "Just the two lowest-ranking ones. The others all have an ego problem; they clash when they are together. They all want to be the boss. They can't just work together to get the job done."

"Maybe it is more efficient for them to keep separated," Vanna suggested.

Gabe gave a half-grin. "Depends on who you talk to. That is Ira's claim but to hear Claw talk, that is just another way for Ira to keep control."

"What do you think?" Telara asked him.

"I try not to; it gives me a headache." Gabe winked at her. "Seriously, I just keep doing my job. Ira doesn't even bother with Tobias or me, so I have no worries. Here we are." He pointed to a tree that was about half the size of the Elder Tree but about the same size as the ones towering around them.

When they first arrived, they had to duck and take cover due to the pots and pans that were flying.

Now, they were watching Gabe who was trying to discover exactly what had started the problem. Mostly, he was holding the two gnome brothers apart so they didn't kill each other.

"If you guys would tell me what the problem is maybe we would be able to fix it," Gabe said through clenched teeth as he grabbed Shirk by the scruff and pulled him away from Tad who was swinging a cooking pot in defense.

"That toad faced brother of mine has no respect for anyone other than himself," Shirk was shrieking.

Tad rolled his eyes. "Always so melodramatic!" He sighed and shook his head.

"Melodramatic? Melodramatic?"

Tad had to duck as Shirk managed to shuck a vase at his head before Gabe was able to snatch it. It would have smashed against the wall except that Telara managed to stop it in midair and let it softly fall to the floor. She stared at the vase that laid on the floor in one piece. She didn't know how she was able to do that.

Shirk stopped his screaming and looked over at them with wide eyes. "You are not normal humans."

Gabe gave a deep sigh still holding onto Shirk. "No, Shirk; they are the Guardians."

Shirk jerked back in surprise. "Really?"

Cole looked at them and smiled as if he figured that with that knowledge the fighting would be over. "Yes, we are."

"Hmmph! Didn't realize that the Guardians had been reduced to menial patrol duty!" Tad grunted.

Chad raised his eyebrows at that. "Menial patrol duty? Hmmm seems to me that this is the most entertainment that I have seen this whole summer."

"Entertainment? You are calling having my property disrespected and vandalized entertainment?"

This time, Shirk's voice was very loud and very screechy. Telara could only shake her head as two vases went flying towards Chad and Cole this time. She tried to concentrate on the vases to cause them to stop, but both vases shattered against the wall behind the two. She growled in frustration over not being able to accomplish the feat twice.

"We're not suggesting that your problem is any less important," Brie went on to assure them as Gabe was too busy holding Shirk back from tearing into both Chad and Cole. Tad leaned back against the table watching the show with delight evident in his eyes.

"My favorite picture being vandalized is not a problem! It is a catastrophe," Shirk informed her very haughtily before hurling yet another vase at the two Guardians who couldn't believe they had become the new target.

Vanna looked at the wall beside her where a picture of two nymphs was crooked. She reached over and straightened the picture then froze as the room went silent. She looked back at the two brothers who were staring at her with very dumbfounded expressions for a split second. They waited for the brothers to start hurling projectiles at her for daring to touch their property. Just as quickly as the fight had started, it had now stopped. The brothers each picked up a broom and started to sweep up the room of the broken vases. The Guardians and the Theta group both looked at each other not sure what to make of this new situation.

"Well, are you gonna just stand there or help us clean up this mess?" Shirk asked them as if he had not been the cause of the said mess.

"Ummm, sure. We can help," Cole said not wanting to be the target of any more stray vases. Almost an hour later, they were leaving the house to finish their patrol with the Theta group.

"I have got to ask exactly where did they get so many vases to throw?" Cole asked.

Gabe and the Theta group chuckled.

"Those two brothers are potters," Gabe explained.

The Guardians groaned at that news. The rest of the patrol was rather boring compared to the brothers' bickering. After all, the Theta group was mainly on watch for Shadows that managed to infiltrate Sanctuary.

Finally, they met up back at Czaar's Cantina to find Pam and the Alpha group there waiting to hear all about their first-ever patrol. Pam was surprised to hear them tell her that they had a great time, and all of them had chuckles over the broth-ers' issues. They had to pull several tables together to accom-modate the Alpha group, the Guardians, and the Theta group. Many members of the Theta group looked uncomfortable sitting with the Alpha group, even after spending the night with the Guardians. Gabe seemed comfortable, as he had the whole night, so it didn't take long before the rest of the group seemed to accept it as well.

There were shouts from the other side of the cantina where the weird-looking game table was. They glanced over and saw a very tall and lanky guy holding up his tankard and laughing. His hair was deep red in color and very spiky. He reminded Telara of a cousin who got the name porcupine head from such a haircut. He glanced over at them, and Telara was taken aback by his very green piercing eyes. She had heard many people describe such eyes and had thought that it was ridiculous to call eyes piercing, but she now amended that thought. It felt as if he was piercing her with his eyes. Then he winked and turned back to his companions.

Telara looked over at Pam who had a smile on her face. "That is Claw." Pam shook her head with a big smile.

"Ahhhh…the abrasive, instigative Scott." Telara grinned, and Pam groaned. The Alpha faction looked at Telara as if she had just lost all her senses.

"Ummm…Did we miss something?" Chance looked from Telara to Pam.

Telara grinned at him. "Nah, I just think maybe we should go introduce ourselves to the Gamma Leader. After all, we just spent the night with Theta; we wouldn't want to look like we are showing favoritism."

Gabe gave Pam a look that clearly said is this girl nuts? Pam just shook her head at him as if to say don't ask. Then to Telara, she said, "I've not known you very long, but I'm thinking that you're not someone I want on my bad side."

Telara grinned at her and then stood up. "You know, I'm very interested in that game they are playing."

Cole gave her a look of surprise. "Telly, you've never been one for table games of any sort."

Telara shrugged. "Didn't say I was going to play it, just that I was interested." She walked over to the other side of the cantina.

"Is she always this unpredictable?" Pam asked Tia in an undertone.

Tia chuckled. "You have no idea. You should've seen when her parents forced her to go to a dance that she did not want to go to."

"Something tells me that it ended up badly," Pam guessed.

"Ever seen the movie Carrie?" Pam shook her head. "Rent it some time," Tia suggested chuckling, and Pam just groaned.

They were standing around the table watching the huge marbles bouncing off the bumpers that were constantly changing colors. Every now and then, a marble would disappear into the bumper it touched, and the table would start to flash colors to the cheers of the onlookers.

"So how is this game played?" Chance asked watching the game with interest.

"Well, follow me people, and I will give you a crash course. But let's not disturb Claw as he tends to get cranky with anyone who disturbs his games," Pam smiled.

Sapphire grunted, "Cranky? Is that what you call putting a man over the bar?"

"I wasn't going to mention that." Pam gave her a half-hearted glare to which Sapphire gave her a cheeky smile. Telara couldn't believe that they were having as much fun hanging out with Pam and the Alphas. If anyone told her from the beginning that they would become friends with Pam, she would have told them they needed to be committed. But these guys were really fun to hang with.

Pam kept her eyes on Claw who was strapping a device to his hand that resembled what the healers used for memory loss. Claw, for his part, was ignoring Cole who was watching the marble disappear into a blue-colored bumper. Claw walked up to the table and, with a flick of his wrist, sent a flashing blue marble into a red flashing one which then disappeared into a blue bumper.

"The object of this game is to hit the opposing player's ball into one of your colored bumpers," Pam explained.

"That sounds easy enough," Cole said not taking his eyes off the table.

"Watch the bumpers," Pam advised and, as they watched, the recently blue bumper suddenly turned yellow. "If you knock the ball into a color that is either theirs or not one of yours, it just reflects the ball back. It is more a game of chance than anything. The bumpers change color very randomly."

"Game of chance ye say?" Claw asked Pam, and you could hear the Scottish accent. "Ye saying there be no skills tae playing this game Alpha Leader? Would ye be saying that because tis a game that yer not that good at?" He asked these questions without taking his eyes off the table or even looking at Pam who just glared at him. "And who be yer companions Alpha Leader?"

"I do have a name you know." Telara could hear the tension in Pam's voice and wondered if there was not more to this than meets the eye.

"Everyone be having a name, Alpha Leader." Claw knocked the last red marble into a blue bumper causing the whole table to light up with blue lights. "But I wouldn't want tae be disrespecting ye by not calling ye by yer title."

"It's not disrespectful to call someone by their name, Claw." They heard the tightness in Pam's tone, and they could feel the tension from the other Alphas standing there. "Good manners are all that is required."

Telara got the feeling that this was most likely how all of Pam's and Claw's meetings were like. There definitely had to be more there than just differences of opinions. Telara wondered if maybe there weren't feelings that were being denied. She looked over at Tia who was having a hard time hiding her smile at that thought.

"You would think even you would be interested in meeting the Guardians," Pam said.

"Manners? I dinna know what they are and as fer the Guardians." He looked them over one by one. "They dinna look like anything special tae me." He looked directly at

Telara. "Hope yer newest accessory disna clash with your outfits."

Telara clenched her teeth together. She could not believe the gall of this man. He knew nothing about them but felt like making comments like that?

"Gee, I guess I should feel special that the green-eyed, porcupine red-haired Scotland reject of Sanctuary is concerned with wee ol' me?" Telara glared at him, deciding that she wasn't going to put up with anyone's flack. Who did he think he was anyway?

Everyone in the room held their breath as Claw stared silently at her. She was sure she had just created a great faux pas, but she didn't care. He looked at them as if they were a bug on the ground, and she wasn't going to take it silently. Claw's face started to soften until he actually smiled and then threw back his head and laughed.

Telara could hear Pam release her breath next to her. "What part of unstable did you not get?" Pam muttered under her breath.

Claw held out his hand to her and, after a brief pause, she took it. "I like ye. The name is Claw."

Telara pursed her lips together. "Hello, Claw. I am Telara, but you can call me Telly if you wish." Telara then motioned to the others. "This is Vanna, Chad, Chance, I.Q., and Tia. The idiot who's trying to figure out where the balls went is Cole."

Cole got up off the floor where he was looking under the table to give her a glare. Claw just chuckled, grabbed his drink off of a neighboring table, walked back to their table, and took a seat.

Telara glanced at Pam. "Makes himself right at home doesn't he?"

"This is one of his good days; actually, I would have to say this would be the best one I have seen. Normally, he tells everyone to get bent then walks out. He must have liked your spunk more than I would've thought." Pam joined Claw at the table, and the others slowly followed.

As time went on, after a full day of training with the Crims and then Raphael, they found themselves preferring the cantina to unwind rather than their own game room. Either they would head there after some time in the Static Room or, if they felt more like socializing than power training, they would head to the cantina instead. They also discovered that Silest made some mean burgers and fries.

They went on a few more patrols with Gabe and the Thetas, but nothing as interesting as the two brothers happened. They met a few more of the townsfolk, who seemed very interested in the new Guardians. It seemed that the reputation of the Guardians was changing with every passing day. After their patrols, they would spend the rest of the night at the cantina where the Alpha group would join them before they strolled off to their bungalow for sleep.

Gabe seemed to have garnered Vanna's attention as she was at his side whenever he was playing Rainbow Ball. Cole even tried to play the game with disastrous results. Gabe explained that you couldn't just whip the balls. This was due to the Crim device attached to the hand that was used in directing the balls.

"It is very sensitive, Gabe explained. "And if you move your hand too quickly, the ball will shoot across the room." This happened to Cole, which almost started a bar brawl with some gnomes and satyrs. Thankfully, one look from Claw calmed them all down, although it made Telara more curious about him.

During one evening, they were all seated around the table

that had become dubbed as the Alpha Guardian table. Tia was listening to Serdita playing her Chenras with her chin resting on the back of her chair. Vanna was in deep discussion with Gabe regarding the last game he had played with Cole and Chad. They were inputting ideas of their own on tactics. Chance was talking with Stella regarding their training session earlier that day. Stella and Chance seemed to get on rather well. Telara hoped that Brom didn't find out about that. Brom seemed to think of Chance as her very own personal mortal. Chance would take early morning swims in the lake with Brom and her sister to keep in practice for swimming season. Brom seemed to think there was more to it, and Telara really hoped that Brom would find a merman before she realized that Chance thought of her more as a sister than a girlfriend.

On the other side of the table, I.Q. was tapping away on the Stargazer, and you could see the case light up every now and then. I.Q. kept his eye out for Claw who was also a regular at Czaar's. Claw seemed awfully interested in the Stargazer after the first time I.Q. let him check it out. While none of them could figure out what the buttons meant or be able to work it like I.Q., Claw had no problem getting it to work for him. Telara was sure that put a dent in I.Q.'s pride, but the biggest problem then became Claw trying to talk I.Q. out of the Stargazer. Claw finally took the hint that it wasn't up for grabs but every time he saw it, the gleam in his eye unnerved I.Q. so much that when Claw would enter, I.Q. would then shrink it down so that it would fit into his pocket.

Telara looked around the room and saw Pam enter and head towards their table. Their training with the Crims was going rather well even if Telara couldn't get her bracelet to do much of anything just yet. The others were almost as good as the Alphas at using theirs...almost. Good enough to get praise from the Alpha leader herself and even get time off early sometimes. Pam didn't give Telara much grief considering her Rotary, as it was called, was considered an enigma. Telara mostly practiced some hand-to-hand combat with Pam...a bit friendlier than the first time they had trained together. If there were only the Guardians and the Alphas in the training room, she would practice with her powers. She never forgot Lucius telling them to be careful of showing off too much in front of others.

She never spoke her thoughts out loud and had even learned to hide certain ones from even her friends. But at times like this, she thought a lot about Gage and how she wished he could be here not only to see this but also be a part of it.

17

———

TELARA LAY on her back in her bed staring at her circle friends racing across the ceiling. She couldn't get herself to fall asleep no matter how hard she tried. She had been tossing and turning for the past hour or so; yet, sleep still eluded her.

Where is Morpheus when you need him?

She curled on her side and stared out the window at the lights that were floating around outside. Her mind was too busy replaying the past week. Her friends had finally managed to work their Crims so well that there wasn't a thing they could not do with them. Heck, they discovered that the Crims not only had their own powers but enhanced their powers as well. Their friendship with Pam was even stronger, and Telara chuckled when she thought about their adventures in the town. She thought about Gabe and their patrols, especially the brothers. The people they had met since coming here had definitely been an interesting lot.

Telara closed her eyes and when she opened them, she saw Bright Eyes looking down at her with a smile.

"Gee, I thought you had decided to give up on me," Telara

told him with a smile. It had been some time since the last dream walk she had had.

"Come with me, please." Bright Eyes held his hand out to her.

"You can speak English?" Telara asked incredulously.

"Please come," he repeated.

"Well, I guess some English is better than none," Telara said and took his hand.

He pulled her up and wrapped his arms around her.

"Hey, haven't you ever heard of personal space?" Telara said and pushed back against him, but he held her tight.

"Close your eyes," he said. Just as he said that, Telara felt the ground beneath her feet disappear, and she grabbed him very tightly around the waist. She heard him grunt and felt a bit of satisfaction. She pressed her face into his chest as she felt air whoosh around her.

We are flying, she realized and closed her eyes very tightly until she again felt the ground. She pushed him away from her as soon as she had her footing and glared at him.

"A little warning would've been nice," she told him then watched as he walked away from her and walked towards the dark building in front of which they had landed.

The building looked as if it had been abandoned for a very long time with broken windows and boards that looked as if they were being held together by sheer will.

"I'm not going in there," she told him, but he kept walking. "Do you hear me? I'm not going into that building." She watched as she saw him walk through the door and gave a growl before following him. "If I fall through the floor, you are so gonna get it," she muttered under her breath.

He turned towards her and held his finger to his lips as if to say shhh. She was about to retort when she realized that the walls were not made of wood but stone. It looked as if they were in the Sanctuary caves except that the sconces here had blue flames rather than the colored crystals. She almost screamed as a Shadow minion brushed up against her, but Bright Eyes covered her mouth and shook his head. Then, he grabbed her hand and pulled her along the hallway. She watched as minions were moving up and down the hallway as if they were not even there.

"So even they cannot see us?" she asked and put her hand over her mouth as she saw a Shadow creature turn towards the direction she was standing. This one was bigger than any minion she had ever seen, and its facial features were a bit more human.

Generals.

SHE LOOKED OVER AT BRIGHT EYES AND REALIZED HE WAS MIND speaking with her.

Can they hear us?

Minions – no. Generals can hear spoken words but not mental.

Why haven't you spoken in English to me before?

Your mind was too closed for me to understand you but now I can. When you speak mentally with someone, you will always be able to understand them. Words spoken out loud are not as easy to under-stand, but I am getting better. Follow me; I have something to show you.

Telara followed him down the hallway, making sure to skirt around the General that was still staring at the spot she had just vacated. Bright Eyes smiled at her maneuver, causing her to stick her tongue out at him.

You know I cannot keep calling you Bright Eyes, so what is your name?

You can call me Zach.

Zach. Telara rolled her tongue around the name. *K and you can call me Telara or Telly.*

I know. Telara could hear the chuckle in her head and gave him a glare that didn't seem to bother him one bit.

They heard a scream come from a room a bit further down the hall. Zach motioned for Telara to follow him into that room, but she held back a bit not sure if she really wanted to step through that doorway. Her palms were sweating, and she was starting to feel very unsure of what they were doing. Finally, she entered the room and gasped at what she saw.

Gage was tied to a rock table that resembled a gurney you would see in a hospital. His arms and legs were held by manacles that were glowing a dark purple. Telara looked at Zach and saw him just watching the proceedings without an expression on his face. She turned back to Gage when he moaned, causing the figure that was standing off to the side to amble over to him. This was no minion; it seemed taller and more human-looking than even the Generals did.

Shadow Maker. Telara felt a shiver run through her when Zach said that; she had a bad feeling this wasn't a good thing.

How many different types of fricken Shadow creatures are there? Telara could feel her irritation rise; she hated not knowing exactly what was going on.

Is one mortal the same? Telara had no answer for that, but she couldn't stop the agitation that was coursing through her.

"Are you ready to work with us now, young one?" the Maker rasped out with his wheezy voice.

"Never!" Gage spat at him, and Telara almost cheered him on if it wasn't for Zach putting a restraining hand on her arm. She looked at him, and he shook his head.

Just because most cannot hear us when we speak out loud during these jaunts of ours, there are many that can, and we cannot risk that.

Like they can hurt me? My body is still in my bed, correct?

Yes, your body is but not your mind.

That stopped the next retort that Telara had and effectively kept her mouth shut. She didn't want to imagine what it would be like if they managed to destroy her while she was out of her body. Her friends might wake up the next morning to a body that was alive and yet not. That made her shiver.

"Well, I guess we will have to step up our process then," continued the Maker in that same wheezy voice that gave Telara shivers.

"Now, now, Jasper. Don't cause the young man any more distress," came a very soothing voice from behind Telara.

The voice startled her very much. In came another Shadow creature with a very feminine outline, although Telara couldn't tell very well since there was a dark cloak wrapped all around it. But the voice was definitely very feminine, although Telara knew that didn't necessarily mean a thing. The creature walked over to where Gage was laying and put a hand, which did indeed look like a woman's hand, on Gage's forehead. Gage tried to pull away from the touch but couldn't.

"Do not stress yourself, my child; this will go so much easier if you would not fight."

Gage spat at the woman who still had not moved, but since they could not see her face due to the cloak, Telara wasn't sure if she showed any emotion or not.

Her voice still sounded very calm and soothing. "No worries; it will be over shortly."

As she again put her hand on his forehead, his face tightened as if he was in great pain and then he let out a scream that pierced through Telara. She couldn't stop herself and before Zach could stop her, she shouted, "NO!"

She couldn't let this happen; she needed to do anything to stop this. As she thought this, her bracelet glowed an eerie blue.

The Maker and the female had turned and looked directly at them as soon as she had yelled, but she didn't care at this point. All she could think about was that her friend was in pain. She held out her hand with the glowing bracelet. As she stared, she saw the bracelet come alive and suddenly lash out to knock the woman's hand away from Gage's forehead. Telara got a good look at the woman under the cloak and was shocked to discover that there was no trace of the dark skin the other Shadow creatures all wore. The woman was beautiful with pale skin, and her eyes were actually a dull blue.

Then a gurgling came from the table, and Telara saw what use to be Gage was now a Shadow creature.

"And so a minion is born," the woman said softly still staring at Telara with that very serene expression.

"Intruders!" the Shadow Maker rasped out. "Find whoever it is and take them to the Master."

"Time for us to leave now; I would say we have overstayed our welcome," Zach said.

Telara looked over at Zach expecting him to be very upset with her, but he just pulled her into his arms. The room disappeared and suddenly they were in a field outside the home of the chosen.

"Why did we leave? We could have saved him!" Telara screamed at him pushing him away from her. Her vision was blurred due to the tears that now were threatening to spill over.

"Not alone we cannot. That is a mistake many chosen have made in the past. Silly me; I thought you were different."

Telara glared at him for that reprimand, hating that there was no argument for that.

"So why did you take me there and show me that if you knew there was nothing we could do?" she asked in a very sulky tone.

"To show you what you are up against."

"Can we help him?"

"They say that the weakest link is always your strongest weapon."

"Yeah, for the bad guys you mean."

Zach smiled at her and leaned down to kiss her softly on the lips. Telara closed her eyes and when she opened them, she was back in her bed.

18

———

"Our strongest weapon is our weakest link?" I.Q. repeated after Telara had told them all about her nightly adventure.

"I tell you I found Gage, and that is all you have to say?" Telara asked.

"Your nightly visitor has always visited you to help you, so yeah, I'm more interested in what could help us in defeating the damn Shadow creatures," I.Q. said glaring at Telara for her outburst. "Because right now even knowing that they are turning Gage into a Shadow creature or whatever isn't going to help us save him if we don't know what to do."

"We know with our powers combined we can create enough light to hurt them…" Cole began only to get interrupted by Vanna.

"We don't want to hurt Gage or now even any other minion. Who says they aren't friends?" she said.

"Let me finish," Cole said with a hint of exasperation in his voice and then glared at Telara who couldn't help but giggle. It amazed her how it seemed as if in only a couple of months they had all seemed to have grown up a lot. "We can create enough light to hurt them but not kill them; maybe enough to stop them and capture them so that we can then find a way to help them."

"But what can we do to help them?" Telara asked. "We don't know anything about the Shadow creatures. Heck, we are just beginning to learn our powers that are a part of us let alone a whole race of creatures whose whole purpose is our destruction."

"Then I guess it is time we learn."

They jerked around to see Pam standing at the entrance to the common room.

"Took you long enough," Telara told her, motioning for her to join them.

"Sorry, but getting a summons to the Guardians residence is such a rare event that I had to make sure that someone wasn't pulling my leg and it was an actual invite," Pam said with a shrug.

"How much did you hear?" Telara asked her.

"Enough to know that my second in command is not as lost as we thought he was," Pam said sitting down in one of the white armchairs. "But I wasn't exaggerating when I said no one has ever been invited here. As a matter of fact, Lucius almost barred my entry until I showed him your letter. As far as I know, I am the only non-Guardian person to have ever stepped into this place, and I am feeling a bit awed by it all," she ended with a bit of a half-grin.

"How did Lucius even know you were here?" Tia asked. "We hardly ever see him around."

"He is the Caretaker," Pam said as if that was the answer to everything. "Anyway, to get back to the matter at hand. How well do you trust this nightly visitor of yours?" She looked directly at Telara.

"He has yet to lead me wrong and has always helped me," Telara told her. "Although I wish he would just tell me exactly what I have to do."

"Yeah, well he sounds like an oracle or something, and they never tell you exactly what you need to know; they just guide you. I can't stand them personally; makes more questions than answers and, in the end, it is not them that saves the day," she said. "So what is our next move?"

Telara smiled at how Pam and her Alphas had seemed to integrate themselves into the group so easily. It was as if those few weeks had never happened.

As it should be, Telara thought. The others smiled in agreement.

Chance shook his head. "We were hoping that you might be able to shed some light for us. Do we wait for the next attack and hope that one of the Shadows is Gage and try to capture as many as we can? Is that even possible?"

Telara looked at Pam. "What do you know about the other Shadows I saw there: the Generals and the Maker?"

Pam shook her head. "We have only dealt with the minions. There might be something in one of the history books regarding the others, but I have no personal experience with them."

Telara leaned her head back and groaned.

Great. More mysteries. Not like we don't have enough with just getting our powers to work right for us. They felt the frustration at that thought.

"Well, let's not worry about those right now," Tia suggested. "Let's concentrate on how to save Gage. Then, we can worry about what other monsters we will have to face."

"Can you remember where this fortress is?" Pam asked Telara.

Telara shook her head. "Sorry, but he just transported us there. And I don't even know how. I hid my face in his shoulder and when I looked up, we were there."

Pam stood up and motioned for them to join her. Cole gave her a quizzical look

"Ummm, we really need to figure out if there is any way to save Gage," Cole said.

Pam glared at him "I do know that, and I have an idea if you will follow me."

Cole looked sheepish but didn't say another word as he followed Pam with the rest of them.

"I have an idea, but I'm not too sure if it will work," she said.

"Well, don't keep us in suspense," Chad told her.

Tia kicked him in his shins. "You could try being a bit less obnoxious than normal," she grumbled glaring at him. Pam grinned at her, but the grin quickly disappeared.

"I'm not too sure how well my idea will work out," she said hesitantly.

"Hey, we are willing to try anything," Cole reassured her trying to make up for his hasty comments of earlier.

"That's not my worry."

They reached the hidden path and started towards Thetis following behind Pam, who seemed to be licking her lips nervously as she continued.

"Remember when I told you Claw and Ira had a falling out?" They nodded towards her, and Telara gave a small smile at the memory.

"Well...the weapons they argued about were not actual weapons." This confused them, and it showed on their faces. "Claw claimed he knew a way to trap the Shadows so that we would be able to find a better way to win this war."

"Ira rejected this idea?" Cole, forgetting that he was trying to stay silent, objected. "What? Did he think without the Shadows he wouldn't have a job? The man would make a great politician." The others were too shocked themselves to shush him, not to mention they were thinking the same thing.

Pam held up her hands. "Before you judge, hear me out." They grudgingly nodded their heads. "In Ira's defense...and he does have one...no one knew the possibility the Shadows we have been fighting were, in fact, our fallen comrades." None of them looked too convinced of Ira's innocence, so Pam went on. "Many years ago, possibly even before Sanctuary came to America, the Gamma faction at that time tried that. The Head of Defense gave them her approval. With that endorsement, they started the Shadow Apprehension Movement, otherwise known as operation S.A.M. It ended in catastrophe... Sanctuary lost over half the population before they were able to defeat the Shadows and re-strengthen their borders. That Sanctuary was double the size of this one with more fighters than we could hope to house here. The Head of Defense lost her life in that battle, and the head of Gamma, Claw's ancestor, was deemed unstable due to that."

Their earlier stubborn faces were now one of shock. The horrors of what Pam was describing shook them. This Sanctuary alone had to house over a thousand or more people, human and mythicals alike. The idea of losing over half of that was indeed a scary thought.

"Now you know why Ira vetoed it."

They nodded.

"But how will we get Ira to agree with it now?" Cole asked.

"Knowing the Shadows could be comrades should be enough," Tia grunted.

Pam shook her head sadly. "I really doubt that."

"So how do we convince him?" Telara asked.

"We don't," Pam said simply. "Don't get me wrong; I think very highly of Ira. If not for him, I wouldn't be where I am. I just don't believe that he will consider the possibility of what could happen worth the risk. But he was the one who taught me to take care of my team and Shadow or not, Gage is still part of my team." This was said very forcefully as if daring them to contradict her.

"So…we go behind his back," Chad mused with a gleam in his eyes that was shared with Cole. "We can handle that."

Pam grimaced as if the thought held no appeal to her.

"So I guess we are going to talk to Claw and have him show us how to capture the Shadows," Vanna guessed.

Telara, who was watching Pam, saw Pam's face tighten. "That isn't going to be too easy is it?" she guessed, and Pam shook her head at her with a grimace.

"Why not?" Chance protested. "Shouldn't he be happy someone wants to hear his ideas?"

Pam gave a wry chuckle. "You don't know Claw very well; he is going to want his pound of flesh first. After Ira dismissed his ideas and ordered him to cease and desist, he came to me asking me to plead his case. I refused; I told him if he wanted to get anywhere, he needed to forget all about the eccentric ideas of his ancestor."

"Ouch!" Cole grabbed his mid-section as if punched. "You don't hold back any, do you?"

Pam grimaced at that comment but nodded as she knew what she had said was indeed harsh. Although, at the time, it seemed appropriate to try to help Claw get back in Ira's good graces. Now, she indeed wished she had handled it differently. They had reached the door to Silest's tavern. Pam took a deep breath before opening the door.

"Here goes nothing or should I say everything."

There at their table, Gabe and Claw were watching a couple of satyrs playing Rainbow Ball.

Pam grabbed a chair, turned it, and then straddled it. She stared at Claw, who didn't even acknowledge their approach.

"You once said you knew a way to capture the Shadows. Were you serious?"

Telara grabbed a chair and sat close to Pam, giving them her utmost attention. The other Guardians followed suit.

Claw looked over at Pam then turned back to the satyrs. "Well now, what would Ira's pet want with just capturing the Shadow creatures rather than trying tae destroy them?" he drawled in his Scottish accent.

"Do you or don't you?" Pam pressed.

"What's it worth to ye?" Claw leaned back in his chair, staring at Pam. "Weren't ye the one who sided with Ira? I believe ye said if I wanted tae get anywhere, I needed tae get all those eccentric nonsense thoughts out of my head."

Cole grimaced at the venom in his voice.

"If you want me to admit I was wrong then fine – I was wrong." Pam emphasized the word wrong.

Claw didn't say anything; he just took another sip of his drink. He didn't seem like he was in the mood to help them. After all, Pam had told them how she and Ira had both scoffed at his ideas. Telara could understand why he wouldn't want to help. But if they had any hope of saving Gage, they would need his help. The big question was whether or not this eccentric was going to help them now or not. He was, after all, the weapons expert and if he could make something out of the crystals that would actually contain the creatures rather than hurt them, they might be able to not only save Gage but also dwindle the creatures' numbers.

"How about we make a bet?" Everyone turned toward Vanna. She hated betting and would be the first to tell the boys off for doing just that.

But she did get Claw's attention. He turned to smile at her and earned a glare from Gabe.

"Well, luv, exactly what bet would ye be making?" That endearment earned him another glare from Gabe. If they weren't in such a serious situation, Telara would find more amusement in that.

"Rainbow Ball," Vanna announced, and Cole looked a bit green. His one try at Rainbow Ball had had them all ducking for cover.

Claw laughed and gestured towards Cole. "What? Is Boy Wonder here actually going tae be able tae keep the balls on the table long enough fer a game?"

"Not Cole; me." Vanna crossed her arms and stared right back at Claw daring him to turn her down in front of the whole bar.

"And the wager?" Claw looked interested at least.

"I win, you help us," she said.

Claw nodded as if that was a given. "And what do I get when I win?"

"The Stargazer."

You could hear I.Q.'s intake of breath when Vanna announced that. Telara had even held her breath as she waited for I.Q.'s denials, but they never came. He didn't even look at Vanna.

Claw jumped out of his chair and grasped Vanna's hand. "Deal."

With that, he walked over to the table and, after a few seconds, the satyrs walked away without so much of an argument. Telara really wondered exactly what it was about Claw that had everyone jumping when he spoke.

"Vanna, I hope you know what you are doing," Telara said under her breath. I.Q. still hadn't said anything, but Telara was sure he would be paying close attention to this game.

"Me, too." Vanna walked up and grabbed her hand piece to get ready to play. With a push of a button, the colored balls appeared on the table.

"Lasses first."

Claw held out his hand, which Vanna ignored. The game would've been hilarious if the stakes weren't so high. The Stargazer held information that I.Q. was sure was very important to them. But Claw's help right now was equally important.

Claw managed to hit two of Vanna's red balls against blue bumpers causing I.Q.'s shoulders to stiffen.

Claw grinned at her. "Ready tae call it quits, luv?"

Vanna just ignored him and managed to hit his blue ball against a red bumper.

Claw was still smiling; after all, he still had seven balls to her six. Vanna lost two more balls, taking her down to four. Claw smiled at a grim-faced I.Q.

"Well, lass, I hope ye have my prize with ye."

I.Q. didn't rise to the bait, and they watched as Vanna took another one of Claw's balls off the table.

Their game had attracted the attention of the whole tavern. Telara heard bets taking place, most in favor of Claw. She heard Gabe putting one in for Vanna, causing a gnome to chuckle at him, Telara might have too if her whole focus wasn't on the game before them.

They were down to one ball each with Vanna up.

"Better be making this one, luv. If not, that box be mine," Claw grinned.

Vanna shot her red ball into his blue ball sending it towards a blue bumper.

Turn Red…Turn Red…Turn Red, Telara kept chanting in her head, not caring if the others could hear her or not.

As the ball neared the bumper, they watched as it turned red right before the ball touched, and the table lit up in red lights.

"WOO HOO! Way to go, Vanna!" Cole yelled picking up Vanna and swinging her around in victory. Vanna's face was red from the intense game, but there was also a big smile. They smiled with her. They could hear the grumblings of all those who had bet against her.

"Serves you all right for betting in the first place," Vanna admonished them.

Gabe had a big smile on his face as he collected his winnings. "Drinks are on me," he proudly proclaimed.

Telara pulled Vanna aside. "When did you learn to play Rainbow Ball?"

Vanna gave her a cheeky grin. "Gabe has been giving me some lessons."

"Not bad," Claw had to grudgingly admit.

I.Q. clapped Vanna on the back and told her good game. They could all see the relief that was evident on his face.

"So what do ye need?" Claw asked.

Claw told them all about how he was able to create a crystal net that would not only ensnare a Shadow but also there was a switch that would then transport the Shadow to any destination specified. The only problem was the material needed for this contraption to work was thought to be hard to work with; that, and never having created a cell to contain the Shadows due to Ira putting a stop on all work.

"So you are telling me that the rebellious Claw listened to Ira and never figured out how to create a cell to contain these Shadows?" Telara had to ask.

"I dinnae say I dinnae figure out how tae do it, just that I wasnae able tae create it," Claw corrected her. "I can do it, but I dinna have the crystals I needed to perfect it."

"What crystals do you need?" Pam asked warily.

"Not really crystals, actually. What I need are the crystal essences," Claw told her, and they watched as Pam's face drained of what color there was.

"Those are considered to be unstable even by you. It was in your report," Pam protested.

"They are unstable," Claw chuckled then motioned towards Telara. "But it seems as if there is someone that is able tae withstand their power."

Telara looked down at her bracelet than back at Pam who was frowning.

"You mean Telara's Crim is made up of crystal essence?" Pam asked.

"Dinnae Ira tell ye that?" Claw laughed. "It was in my report. I thought ye got all the reports?"

"So did I," Pam muttered then looked around the room. "So exactly how do we acquire this essence that you need and make these cages without getting caught?"

Gabe walked up to them. "I guess we could always ask the Omega group for help with that."

"What do you mean?" Pam looked at him.

"They have their own barracks that no one uses," Gabe said with a wink. "I am sure they wouldn't mind getting in on this adventure."

Gabe's assumption proved to be very accurate. The Omega leader and group was more than willing to participate in the adventure. They offered their barracks for the cages to be created in without letting anyone in the Command Center in on their plans. Claw had a gnome friend who brought them several carts full of crystal essence that would be used in creating the nets and cages to hold the creatures.

Apparently, the essence was condensed enough that it would not harm the creatures but also had enough power that they would contain them.

"There has never been anyone at Sanctuary that could control the essence enough to use it," Claw grinned then looked right at Telara. "But we now have our very own essence pet."

Telara stuck out her tongue at him not caring if it made her look childish. She wasn't too fond of his nickname for her.

Telara's bracelet seemed to attract the essence as a magnet would metal shavings. With much concentration, Telara could release the essence over the crystals that Claw had set out. Then, the crystal would glow. They watched as the essence would imbue itself with the crystal. This caused the crystal to become more pliable, Claw explained. With heavy gloves on, Claw would forge the crystals into metal rods. He showed them the two crystal buttons on the handle that now encased the whole crystal: one to release the net that would then be attracted to the nearest Shadow creature; the other would transport the creature to the set cage. These cages were made with metal bars that contained crystal essences inside of them. They were safe to touch, but the Shadows wouldn't be able to pass through the metal.

It was now time to test that theory.

When the Delta group announced that there was a Shadow

breach on the north side of town, the Omegas, Thetas, Alphas, and Guardians all went to try out their new plan. The nets that Claw had created would extend out and completely ensnare any Shadow that came within the vicinity. Then they would push the button in the middle of the handle, and the creature inside would transport to the cage to which it was specified. The net would then recoil back into the cylinder until the next time.

The Omegas would be the bait; as soon as a creature would grab one of them, a Theta would use the net and transport the creature. The Alphas were keeping the creatures from getting too far into Sanctuary. After the fifth creature was captured, the others disappeared, leaving all the factions there tired and sweaty but with a feeling of great accomplishment.

19

―――――

TELARA and the others were running through the Command Center looking for Pam amongst all the people running around in white coats. They found her talking to Ira by the porter, and she was all in gear. From the tones of their voices, it was apparent that they had been arguing.

"That was an unauthorized mission. Do you realize how many lives could have been lost?" Ira was glaring at her, ignoring the lights and sirens.

"What is the problem, Ira?" Pam glared at him; one of her patented glares that Telara was glad was not directed at her. "The fact that we didn't bring it to your attention or the fact that it worked?"

Ira's face went completely white. "That was uncalled for. I have always had the best interests of the troops."

"Sometimes the best intentions are not always right." Pam was a bit more gentle. "Please, can we discuss this after we take care of the current problem?"

Ira was standing very stiffly. "So you plan to use these unauthorized and untested contraptions?"

"Yes, we plan to use these unauthorized and semi-tested contraptions." Pam gave Ira an imploring look. "If there is a way to stop all this senseless killing then we need to do it."

Ira sighed and looked at her with tenderness. "Okay." He smiled. "You have my authorization but don't be upset if the outcome isn't what you wanted."

Pam smiled at him gratefully. "I won't, but I'm very positive that you'll be proud."

"I'm already that." He then looked at them as they stood there not sure exactly what to say. The sirens started to get louder as they stood there.

"What is going on?" Telara yelled to be heard above all the wails of the sirens and lights that were flashing all around.

"Sanctuary is under attack," Pam told her. "There is a whole army of minions that have breached our defenses."

Pam's crew was assembling. They were all geared up and ready for the attack. Behind them were many others.

"The whole force is being assembled for this; the civilians have all been evacuated and are hiding in the caves, but I am not sure how well they will be protected there."

"Send them to the bungalow," Telara told her. Ira looked at her as if she had lost her mind.

"N-n-no one but the Guardians are allowed there," he stammered.

"It is the safest place here, correct?" Telara asked him to which he nodded very slowly. "Okay then send them there and tell Lucius to make room. That way, we can battle without having to worry about any innocents."

Telara nodded to the others, and they went and garbed up for what was looking to be the battle of their lives. She wasn't sure how much trouble she would be getting into over this with Lucius but right now she was more worried about keeping everyone safe. She would deal with the consequences later.

They met Pam back by the porter and watched as more troops were being transported to Sanctuary's boundaries to defend against the incoming creatures.

"I think we pissed them off," Pam said looking at Telara. "Wouldn't you agree?"

Telara smiled. "I would. I would also have to say that I am betting there is a way to cure the Shadow creatures. After all, why else would they take such a chance in attacking Sanctuary in this way?" She looked back at Pam. "We just have to survive this and then find the cure."

"You do realize that there is a chance we might not survive this attack?" Pam asked her as they walked towards the porter together.

Telara nodded towards her, not chancing her voice to say anything. The very same thought was going through her mind and by the looks on her friends' faces, they shared their thoughts. Telara thought of her parents and sister back home, who knew nothing of what they were facing. If they died today, what story would Lucius tell their parents? She thought about the last night at home when her mom was upset because she had missed family night; she went out with her friends instead. If they made it through this fight, she would make sure that she never again missed a family night at home. She looked up at the ceiling of the porter.

If anyone up there can hear me, please help us through this night.

"Well, if it means anything, I feel honored to be fighting alongside you guys," Pam said staring straight ahead.

"Well, we feel the same and just so you know, I'll be reminding you of those words after this battle." Telara was just as sure that they would all survive the battle.

"I hope you are right."

They put on their dark glasses as the light of the porter transported them to the outside of the Command Center. They could see the battle had already commenced. Pam started shouting orders to her team to capture as many creatures as they could if at all possible but not at the cost of their own lives. The latter was heavily stressed, and many were clutching their net throwers. You could see their white knuckles clutching the handles.

Telara and Tia went after some minions that had managed to outnumber a member of the Omega team. With a flick of her wrist, Tia's whip (that was already glowing brightly) wrapped around one of the minion's arms, causing it to cry out with pain. Yet, it still held on to the Omega with its other clawed hand. Telara looked down her arm to see her bracelet glowing brightly just like in her dream walk. She flung out her arm and commanded the bracelet to wrap around the other arm of the minion, effectively pulling it away from the Omega screaming in pain. A Theta member had come up and trapped the minion in the lighted netting. He then pressed the button on the handle, effectively transporting the minion to the safe cell. After managing to capture the other three minions, the Omega smiled shakily at them and then took off for the next set of minions, throwing the light bombs to scatter them.

"This seems way too easy if you ask me," Tia said a bit breathlessly, standing next to Telara. Telara was looking out at the chaos that had erupted in Sanctuary.

"I know what you mean," Telara said watching as Cole, Chance, Chad, and I.Q. managed to deflect some of the minions away from Omegas so that the Thetas could net them. Pam and her Alphas were having pretty much the same results as minion after minion was captured and transported. Telara hoped that Claw had built enough cages and that they would be able to contain the number of minions being transported.

"Something is not right. Where are the Generals like I saw with Zach? All I see are minions, and they aren't even attempting to attack Sanctuary, just the fighters," Tia said.

Telara looked over at Tia as a horrible realization dawned. "This is a diversion. The bungalow!"

They realized with horror exactly what was happening. Telara had sent all the mythicals to the bungalow, a magical essence smorgasbord.

Telara radioed Pam telling her what she believed to be happening. Pam couldn't help but agree with her. She told her that they needed to head there and that she would join them as soon as possible.

Guys! This is just a distraction! We need to get to the bungalow and protect all the mythicals there.

The others pulled away from their battles and nodded towards Telara and Tia.

As they approached, they saw Raphael battling with a Shadow creature. There were other centaurs, satyrs, nymphs, and gnomes fighting with Shadow creatures of different sizes and shapes. Telara stared. Some resembled the General that she had seen with Zach, but others were definitely different than the minions who looked like the dark oversized trolls and the General that Telara had seen.

"What are they?" Cole asked.

"Invaders that need to learn manners," Telara said staring around at the chaos.

There were Shadow creatures of all different sizes trying to invade the bungalow. Brom and her sisters were throwing weeds from the lake that resembled nets at Shadows that were daring to approach her home. Several fighters went to her defense before the creatures could do any damage to them. They managed to net one of the minions, but the other two disappeared into the shadows. Flash and several of her brethren were flitting around some of the creatures that had trampled through their fields and throwing exploding bags of pollen that had the creatures stumbling over each other.

"Yippee-Ki-Aye!" They saw a small little guy about the size of a baby doll riding around in what looked like a toy car. He had very wild red hair that spiked straight up, and his face looked as if painted for war. Telara wondered for a brief minute if he was a relative of Claw. She tried to yell at him to be careful as he sped around the feet of a very large giant Shadow that was lumbering towards the bungalow. She watched as he crashed into the feet of one of the minions, who turned and ran after the little guy. Before he was able to catch him, a Theta captured it with a net. Telara breathed a sigh of relief.

Elma and a few other wood nymphs were creating havoc with minions who were attempting to take off with several of their friends. They would cause roots to rise up beneath their feet and creep up their legs, giving their victims the seconds needed to escape.

Tad and Shirk had even joined in; they were pitching their vases at any creature they could see. Brie was taking advantage of this distraction by using her net to capture more Shadows.

So much for coming to their rescue. She grinned at the others, who were all smiling.

"C'mon laddies and lassies!"

They turned to see Claw riding astride a centaur with his Crim that resembled an ax that an ancient Scotsman would be brandishing. Telara smiled as she thought how appropriate it looked for him.

"Let's take these Plonkers!"

Telara looked over at her friends, who were just standing there not sure what to do next.

"You heard the man! Let's take these plonkers!"

With that said, they grinned and, with a shout, they joined the battle.

Telara tried to take out a minion that had a gnome by the foot and was tossing him up in the air. Her light whip wrapped around the leg but as hard as she pulled, she could not pull its leg back. Instead, she used her whip to grab the gnome and yank him out of the creature's hand, causing the gnome to barrel towards the ground. Telara screamed. She ran towards the gnome, knowing she was way too far away to catch him. Telara stopped in her tracks as she saw the gnome come to a sudden stop in midair about one foot above the ground. She looked at her wrist and saw her bracelet glowing an eerie bluish-green color. Then, the bracelet went back to the bluish crystal color, and she heard the thump of the gnome hitting the ground.

"The crystals enhance our powers," she murmured to herself then felt something heavy knock her to the ground.

Looking up, she saw the giant Shadow creature lift its foot as if to step on her as you would a bug on the ground. Telara concentrated with all her might, holding up her arms as if to ward off a blow. She watched as her crystal glowed brightly as the foot neared her. She could hear the screams from her friends telling her to run, but she was done with running. She was done with being scared of the unknown, of not being good enough. Dammit! She was ready to fight back. The foot stopped inches from her as if stopped by an invisible force. Telara held her hands out and concentrated on pushing the foot back. She watched with some satisfaction as the foot was pushed back slowly at first then with more momentum. This caused the giant Shadow creature to fall back, almost crushing a tree nymph that was using her powers to have the tree roots all attack the creatures that were invading her home. If not for Cole thrusting her out of the way, she would not have been able to move in time to avoid the Shadow creature as it crashed onto the ground just inches from them.

Telara stood up and looked over to where the creature laid on the ground not moving. Everyone was cheering, and they started attacking the others with renewed force and conviction.

What was that?

Telara smiled over at I.Q. who was watching her with a very quizzical look.

The crystals only enhance our powers.

With that said, she went after the next giant. She leaped into the air, shocking them all as she landed on the shoulder of the giant closest to her. Not used to being able to jump that high, she almost lost her balance. However, she grabbed onto the giant's ear and righted herself. Amazingly, it seemed as if the giant didn't even notice that she had landed on its shoulder let alone used his ear as a handle. It still kept walking towards the bungalow intent on destruction. The giant reached out its long arms to grab the limbs of the mighty tree and started to pull back. You could hear the groan from the tree as the giant yanked back trying to pull it from the very ground in which it resided.

"NO!"

Telara could hear Vanna scream from down below as this mighty giant again yanked against the tree. Suddenly, you could hear the sounds of something being yanked out of the ground, and Telara feared that Vanna's room was about to be separated from the cave. But as she looked down at the tree, she saw that it was still in the ground without so much as a root showing. She felt the giant jerk itself back and again used its ear for support. She looked down and noticed that roots had begun to wrap themselves around the giant's legs and were slowly creeping upwards. She looked at Vanna and saw her staff glowing just as Telara's bracelet had. She saw the glowing energy seeping into the ground. The giant still had his hands clutching the tree, so Telara ran down the arm of the giant and jumped onto a branch. She turned around. It seemed as if this time the power was there as if it had always been there, just waiting like an old friend for her to find it. She sent out an invisible force to push back at the giant causing him to loosen his grip on the branches. Tia started swinging her whip around her head like a lasso causing the wind to pick up and center directly on the giant. One of his hands released its grip, and the tree swayed back. Telara had to grab a branch for support which dropped the invisible force pushing back at the giant who again tried to reach for the tree. Telara managed to throw up a shield preventing the giant from grasping the tree yet again.

Chance jumped up, swung his flail, and knocked the arm that still had a hold of the tree back with a ball of water that sent drops of water everywhere. Chad and Cole both jumped up on the arm, Chad thrust his sword in the arm, effectively encasing the arm in ice. Cole swung his fiery nunchucks before connecting with the arm. Chunks of icy giant flew out, and they both fell to the ground. The tree, freed from the giant, swung back with Telara still clutching it and holding up her shield as losing an arm still had not stopped the giant.

There was a swishing sound as if something was flying

towards the air, and they saw one of I.Q.'s electrical arrows hit the giant in the center of the chest. Electrical currents could be seen racing around the giant's body before the giant stopped moving and fell backward, causing many to run and take cover.

"Arrgghhh!"

They turned to see Vanna wrestling with a minion. The minion had grabbed onto her staff, putting them in a bit of a tug of war over the staff. Vanna had her hands gripping the base and top of the staff with her legs planted firmly. She practically growled at the minion who was trying to wrench it out of her hand.

"We want to help you, you idiot! Do you want to remain a slave to the Shadows for the rest of your life?"

Telara took off with a leap to help out her friend with the others joining them. Before they reached Vanna and the struggling minion, they saw Vanna's staff start to glow. And right before their eyes, they saw the glowing creep up the minion's arms until it was completely encased in the glow. They heard its screams of agony before it let go of the staff and slumped to the ground.

"You okay?" Telara asked Vanna as they reached her, but Vanna was too busy staring down at the ground and didn't answer. Telara looked down to where Vanna was staring so intently and there on the ground laid Gage. She turned to look at the others with a very stunned look on her face.

"How?" Telara asked.

"Our weakest link is our strongest weapon," I.Q. said with a smile.

"But Vanna is not our weakest link," Telara protested.

"In some people's eyes, her compassion and unwillingness to hurt others would be considered a weak link," he said.

Then, when he saw the look on Telara's face, he hastened to add, "Not that any of us believe that."

"Quit growling at everyone, Telara. You know they are right," Vanna said smiling. She then walked over to the nearest Shadow giant that lay motionless on the ground.

"Careful Van," Telara told her but didn't go to pull her away.

Vanna just smiled at her then touched the end of her staff to the giant on the ground. Again, the glow encompassed the giant on the ground and when it dispersed, they saw a stone giant laying there – minus a hand. She then went over to the other one and repeated her actions.

"Automatons," Pam breathed startling them as they hadn't heard her approach. Telara turned and saw her kneeling on the ground next to Gage. "That is where the missing Automans have gone. So now we know how to defeat them." She looked at the others. "Can you all do that?"

"I don't think so," I.Q. said. "I think that is our own mother nature's specialty." He grinned at Vanna who seemed to be a bit sheepish after this latest discovery.

"So now we have a way to defeat them but only one of you is capable of doing this," Pam breathed.

"One is more than enough."

They turned to see Lucius standing outside the bungalow grinning at them.

"Gee, great time for you to show up after the battle is over," Telara told him with a grin plastered on her face.

Lucius shrugged. "You guys had it all under control." The man had an answer to everything. Now, he just needed to explain his comment. "If you would all join me in my office, I will see if I can answer your questions."

They started into the bungalow after Lucius. Telara turned

around and saw Pam was still standing by the fallen automatons.

"Are you coming?" Telara asked.

Pam looked startled before quickly smiling and nodding. She turned to Sapphire who was helping them put Gage onto a stretcher.

"After you make sure Gage is taken care of, help the Thetas and Omegas with the cleanup. You can let the Betas know they are also expected to help. I would like this done before morning," Pam instructed Sapphire. Sapphire nodded towards Pam then followed the stretcher back towards the Command Center.

20

ALMOST AN HOUR LATER, they had filled Lucius in regarding all that had happened including her dream walking with Zach. Not once during the story had they seen Lucius show even a bit of surprise. It was as if he seemed to already know. Telara said as much when they were done with their story and, to her surprise, Lucius just smiled.

"There is not much that happens here that escapes my eye," he told her still smiling in that benign way that was actually starting to grow on her rather than irritate her as it had in the beginning.

"So why did you not say anything?" Tia asked.

"Considering the Caretaker is the one who was supposed to be leading the chosen," Pam interjected having gotten over the awe of being in the bungalow during her first visit, which now seemed like such a long time ago rather than weeks.

"The Caretaker's job is to guide the Guardians not lead them," Lucius informed them still smiling. "You seemed to be doing just fine on your own, but I promise you if I was needed

I would have stepped in. Now, I'm sure that you have many questions that need to be answered."

"Yeah but are we gonna get answers or just more riddles?" Telara asked with a grimace. At his raised eyebrows, she was quick to defend her outburst. "You can't deny that most of our questions have been answered with more riddles than actual answers."

Lucius smiled. "I guess we will just have to see."

"Okay, I have a question then," Vanna spoke up. When Lucius nodded for her to continue she asked, "Why when we haven't been able to control our power before did it come so easy today? I didn't even have to think, and it came to me without problems."

"You already answered your own question," she was told.

Telara gave a groan and muttered, "Yup, I knew it! More riddles."

"No, not riddles," Cole piped up with a very excited gleam in his eyes. "We didn't think; it just came to us."

"Very good, Cole." Lucius looked rather impressed, but the others in the room started to get irritated.

"Think about it," Cole continued. "When we kept trying to think about how our powers would work, they didn't. But when we just used them, we controlled them."

"Exactly. It is the same as breathing; you do it on a daily basis without thinking about it. But stop to think about how to breathe." They did, and they realized that they had paused in their breathing when thinking about it. Lucius then turned to Chance. "And when you are swimming, do you think about how to do it?"

"No. If I did, it would make me pause and cost me the meet," Chance said. That was when they started to realize what Lucius was telling them.

"Your power is a part of you and always has been. I knew it would come to you when you were ready, not before."

"So that was why you were more worried about training us to fight rather than use our powers," Vanna said slowly.

"Yes. Your powers needed no training; you just needed the confidence to use them," Lucius told them leaning back in his chair with his fingers tapping softly against one another awaiting the next question.

"I have a question," Pam said staring at Lucius with no more of the awe they had seen from her the first time she had come here. Lucius nodded for her to continue. "You said that one was more than enough. What did you mean by that?" They turned to look at Lucius as this was something they had wondered.

"You will only need one with the power to heal the Shadows," Lucius explained. "But as to how that is to be done will depend on the decision of the Guardians." He looked at them and asked, "I once told you that your fate was in your hands and the decision will be yours alone."

"Can we stay here if we wanted to?" Cole asked.

Lucius nodded. "It wouldn't take much to transform Sanctuary from a summer camp to a learning institution to which any parent would be proud to send their children."

"And us getting a free pass?" Tia guessed with a smile.

Lucius nodded. "Of course! Your proficiency with the teachings here have by far surpassed that of any that has been seen for many years and in doing so, you have procured your position in receiving a full scholarship in our program."

They thought about their time here at Sanctuary. After all, here they were almost gods and goddesses. In the real world, they were just average awkward teenagers. They thought about the patrols, their friends at the cantina, their static room, the Crims, and even their training with Raphael. That had become part of their daily life. To give all that up to go back to sitting in a classroom learning math, history, and other teachings paled in comparison to the future that awaited them here. Then there were the friends they had made during their time here. Telara looked over at Pam who was watching them intently, wondering what their decision would be.

Then she remembered her promise before the fight tonight: that she would never miss another family night at home. That promise would be hard to keep if they stayed here. All the training that Chance had put into his swimming would mean nothing. I.Q., who had been working hard on a new electronic game that he planned to unveil at this year's science fair, would never finish. Tia had spent the better part of last year convincing them all to sign up for the volleyball tournament held at the local center. There was so much they had planned for this year that they would have to give up if they stayed.

"The past Guardians were abandoned by those that were supposed to love and take care of them."

They turned to look at Telara, wondering where she was going with that line of thought.

"All they really knew was their life here at Sanctuary. They were treated as heroes and maybe that was their right as that is what they were supposed to be. But they also didn't know how to work with others or see others as equals."

"Hence the rep that they were very anti-social," Chad agreed.

Telara nodded. "But we were lucky; we grew up with our loved ones to look out for us. They overlooked the peculiarities that surrounded us and loved us for us. We were taught values and even humility, but we still have a lot to learn. I don't believe that we could have accomplished what we did today without those teachings. I think we owe it to our families and loved ones to spend as much time with them as is possible." Telara looked at her friends who were all nodding in agreement.

Pam chuckled. "You are willing to give up the fame of being the Great Guardians to go back to being normal teenagers?"

"I think we can do without that fame in all honesty," Vanna told her. "It seems that fame did nothing for the past Guardians." They nodded their heads in agreement.

"I told you that I knew of your existence for many years but chose not to intervene as you were living happy shadow-free lives with your families. I chose to let you live as much a normal life as possible," Lucius informed them with a smile. "I was criticized for not pulling you into Sanctuary as soon as you were discovered so that you would be able to master your powers sooner." Telara remembered Pam telling her about Ira being upset over them coming to Sanctuary so late in life. "I will admit I often wondered if I was doing the wrong thing but looking at you all here now…" He looked from each of them and even to Pam. "I feel I made the right decision."

They felt their faces go a bit warm at Lucius' compliment.

"So how are we going to be able to heal the Shadows that we have captured if they go home?" Pam asked.

"Ahhhh…yes." Lucius stood up and walked over to a cabinet, taking out a clear crystal on a wooden pedestal. "Vanna, if you would please place your hand on the crystal." Vanna looked hesitantly at the crystal and to her friends.

"Go ahead; it won't hurt you," Lucius assured her. She placed her hand on the crystal. "Now, I want you to remember when you placed your staff on the Shadow giant and healed him."

They watched as the clear crystal gave a very light green glow. Lucius then placed the crystal on the corner of his desk and faced Pam.

"You will have this taken to Claw and inform him that he will need to make a new set of Crims, just for healing the Shadows from this parent crystal."

"But how?" Pam stared at the new parent crystal.

"My dear, did you really believe all the parent crystals just appeared with all that power within them?" Lucius smiled. "They all had to be formed from the powers of previous Guardians. Although, there was never one that was created to heal the Shadows before." He smiled down at Vanna.

"So how are we gonna keep on training if we go home?" Cole asked. "I mean, I don't think the Shadows are gonna just drop out of sight until we graduate and have time to train."

"There is always next summer," Telara said.

"I don't think we should just wait until next summer to train," Chance protested.

"You will leave that up to me. You just worry about your schooling," Lucius told them.

"What about our crystal weapons?" Chad asked holding up his crystal that grew into the sword and glinted with the light. "I mean, they'll be kinda hard to carry these around with us to school."

"I really don't think we will need to take these to school with us." Tia shook her head then looked over at Lucius. "Will we?"

Lucius smiled at her. "I believe your friend Claw has some going-away presents for you that will help you out with that. You should really make sure to visit with him before you leave."

"So I guess this is goodbye," Telara stated, feeling a bit saddened by the thought.

Pam clapped her on her shoulder. "Here at Sanctuary we never say good-bye. We just say see ya later." They grinned. "Besides, you guys are not leaving for two more days. We can finish cleaning up tonight, and tomorrow night we will throw you a going away party."

"Woot! Party!" Cole hooted.

"Clean up first," Lucius reminded him.

21

———

Clean up took all night and into the morning as there were many trees and buildings around Sanctuary that had been attacked. Vanna and the wood nymphs helped with trees that had been uprooted and grass that had been torn up. When they got to the bungalow, Vanna's tree was still leaning precariously; it was definitely a sight to see. Vanna and the nymphs surrounded the tree, kneeled down, and put their hands on the ground. The circle seemed to start to glow slowly until you could not see any figure but a circle of light. The tree righted itself, and you could see the roots lower themselves back into the ground until the tree looked as it had on their first day here.

"Mother nature hmmm?" Telara turned to see Gabe staring at Vanna with interest. She chuckled at him. "What?" he asked her.

"Nothing," Telara hastened to assure him. "Yes, she is our mother nature. Always has been and now I can definitely understand why."

"Don't look much like a weak link to me," he said still watching her.

"Me either," Telara agreed. "Well, it looks like clean-up has been taken care of."

Telara looked all around at the lake, forest, and grounds that only hours before had had the biggest battle of her life take place. Although she knew there was a bigger battle that was yet to take place, she couldn't help but feel relieved that this one was over. She just hoped that they could all survive the battle; no one had said anything, but she couldn't stop the feeling of foreboding anytime she thought of the battle with the Magine.

"Yeah," Gabe agreed then turned away. "Well, guess I will see you tomorrow at your going away party."

The going away party was bigger than any party that Telara could ever remember. It took place in the grassy field outside of the bungalow. No need for tents as the sun was about to set anyways. Everyone had slept in due to their late-night cleaning. Gage was still in recovery and was unable to attend the party, which was disappointing as they had hoped to see him before they left. Pam promised that as soon as he recovered, they would be getting in touch. That made Telara feel a bit better. But without him there, it still felt as if something was missing.

There were lights strewn through the trees around them. The nymphs had also put many decorations through their trees that twinkled in the firelight. They had a huge bonfire going that was cooking the meat that the gnomes were all tending. The mermaids had supplied fish for those who did not eat meat. They also had many floating lights bobbing up and down on their lake, although it looked more like they were playing with the lights. Satyrs were helping with the refreshments, well in between chasing a nymph here and there. Telara chuckled. Some things will never change. She leaned back against the elder tree and closed her eyes.

"Well, this is definitely an improvement to the doom and gloom look."

Telara smiled up at Raphael as he joined her on the grass.

"You really seem to like this spot."

Telara looked out over the water and at the bobbing lights. "It is definitely peaceful here."

"You did well." Raphael surprised her with that news. She didn't think he had it in him to compliment anyone. "I do know how to give praise where it is deserved, you know."

"Well, I guess so. I am kind of sad about the thought of leaving everyone here. Finally made some good friends and now it is back to being normal," Telara grimaced.

"Normal?" Raphael raised his eyebrows.

"Yeah, you know no longer a Guardian just a regular person who goes to school, puts up with idiots there, and does homework." Telara definitely wasn't too enthused with the idea.

Raphael just grinned. "I wouldn't hold my breath on your life going back to normal if I was you."

Before she could ask him what he meant by that, he had already galloped off to talk to another centaur that Telara had never seen before. Then again, before last night, Raphael was the only centaur that she had seen here. There was still so much to discover here, but they had a plane reservation tomorrow to take them back to the outside world.

"You do realize that this party is for all of the Guardians?" Pam seemed to come out of nowhere, causing Telara to jump. "Sorry," Pam chuckled not sounding sorry at all.

"Yeah, I guess I'm just not ready to say goodbye yet."

Telara watched as Chance sat on a rock on the shore of the lake to talk with Brom. Vanna and Tia both were talking with some nymphs by the trees and moving a decoration or two. I.Q. was actually in conversation with Claw, and the Stargazer was nowhere to be seen. Of course, after Claw's reaction to it, I.Q. wasn't as keen to have it on him at all times. It was probably stowed away in one of his suitcases. They had all gone down to the Static room for one last time before joining the party. I.Q. had grabbed his Stargazer, Cole had refused to leave without the power ball, and Telara and the others had each grabbed a book from the library. It seemed they all wanted to take a piece of their haven with them.

"I told you…" Pam started to say.

"Yeah, I know. We don't say goodbye, just see you later," Telara interrupted her. "But the question is for how long?"

"Might be sooner than you think." Pam smiled a very mysterious smile. Before Telara could ask what she meant, Pam grabbed her hand and pulled her up. "Come on, girl! Time to join your party."

Telara laughed and let her pull her all the way to the table upon which all the food was heaped. Telara was amazed that it was able to withstand the weight of all the food.

"There ya be, pet."

Telara turned around to see Claw walking up to her and Pam with the other Guardians following closely behind.

"Now don't be trying to leave before I can give ye all yer going away presents."

Telara looked over at Pam who just shrugged her shoulders as if to say she didn't know what he had in mind either.

"Let me be seeing yer Crims now," he told them pulling on a leather glove.

They each held out their Crims for him. He put his gloved

hand into a bag and pulled out several crystal marbles. He took a marble and held it up to each of their Crims. They watched as their Crims glowed brightly, absorbing the marble as they glowed.

Vanna's Crim glowed and started to change form. They watched as it wrapped itself around her waist, forming a very intricate belt of metal and crystal.

"Static!" Cole said.

They then watched as his Crim glowed and wrapped itself around his neck to become a necklace of silver with a red flame crystal hanging from it. Tia's wrapped itself around her forearm to become metal bands with crystal lines woven in. I.Q's became a wristwatch of metal with crystal hands and numbers, with the correct time. Chad's Crim surrounded his finger to become a silver ring resembling a senior ring with an ice blue gem in the center; the designs around the ring showed centaurs and satyrs fighting with Shadow creatures.

Chance's crystal glowed like all the others but then disappeared, causing them to gasp and look around to see where it went to. Vanna gasped, pointing to Chance's ear. There, they saw a single crystal embedded in his ear.

"Mom and dad are going to flip," Chad said holding his sides as he started to laugh with gusto.

"I don't know; I think it looks rather good on you," Vanna told him leaning her head to the side to admire it. "And this you can wear while you are swimming. I have seen many of the other swimmers with the same thing. I thought it was some kind of swimming thing for a while," she giggled.

Telara held up her wrist, and Claw placed the last marble against the ever-moving crystal. They watched as the crystal glowed as it consumed the marble but then went still.

"Mine didn't change." She looked up to Claw who just smiled.

"Yers need no camouflage," Claw told her with a wink.

"So why even add one of the balls to mine then?"

"The balls be more than just a camouflage; they are also my very own version of communication."

"Communication?" I.Q. asked looking down at his watch with curiosity.

"Well, I figured ye all would be going home shortly, so I thought of a way for ye to keep in contact with all yer mates here at Sanctuary."

Claw handed an earpiece to Pam that reminded them of the new hearing aid devices they saw in commercials: very tiny and hard to see when placed in the ear.

Pam put hers in. "Now what?"

"Now one the Guardians need tae be saying yer name," Claw told her.

"Pam," Telara said smiling at Claw who just grinned back.

"I heard you through the earpiece," Pam gasped.

"That way ye can keep in contact with us here at Sanctuary in case ye come into any trouble in the outside world," Claw explained. "They are not easy tae make so only certain people will be getting them but for now Pam, myself, and Lucius will be having one."

"Not Ira?" Telara asked cheekily.

Claw's looked darkened. "No, pet. Not Ira."

The rest of the night was more of a blur as they drank, ate, and generally enjoyed themselves. Telara was talking with Sapphire when she felt as if someone was watching her. She looked around expecting to see one of the dark figures that usually are present with such a feeling. She was very surprised to see Zach standing by the trees. She had never seen him except for in her dreams, so she didn't think he was real. She gave a smile and waved for him to join her, but he just gave her a sad smile.

"Who you waving at?" Tia asked.

Telara looked at Tia and pointed over to where Zach stood. "Don't you see..." But as she watched, he gave her a small wave before disappearing altogether.

"See who?" Tia looked in the direction to which Telara had pointed.

"Nothing I guess," Telara said with a small smile.

"Another one of our stalkers?"

Telara shook her head. "No, just a friend coming to say goodbye."

Tia just shook her head and then pulled Telara back to the party.

The following morning, they were very sad to leave but promised that they would make sure to give everyone a shout. It seemed that each leader of the factions had an earpiece so that they were able to be reached. Of course, Carmen informed them that she would probably be too busy for menial conversation so to make sure if they contacted her it was an emergency. As if she would be the one they would contact but, to keep the peace, they just smiled at her and agreed. They still hadn't met Zeke but were informed he would also be given an earpiece.

Telara and the others gave everyone hugs and waved goodbye as the car drove them away from their newfound home.

Lucius stood in his office staring into the now deserted Static room. It had only been a few hours since the new Guardians had departed and already he missed them. He shook his head.

"Lucius, my friend, you are getting soft in your old age," he said to himself then chuckled.

"I would have to agree with that sentiment, but I would also add that that would not be a good thing considering."

Lucius turned around to greet the man who stood by the door in his dark trench coat. The man didn't offer any greetings nor did Lucius who just went and sat down behind his desk.

"To what do I owe this honor?" Lucius asked in such a way as to imply that it was an honor that he could do without.

The dark-haired man walked over to the window to the same spot that Lucius had just abandoned. He looked down into the Static room without any expression then turned back to look at Lucius.

"Do you plan to tell them the truth of their ancestry?"

Lucius sighed. "I will do what I must to defeat the Shadows and if telling all I know will do that without any deaths, then I will do what I must."

The man glared at him. "This is a foolhardy endeavor you are attempting, old friend. The other gods will eventually learn of their existence if you are not careful."

Lucius stared right back at him with a very serene expression. "You still owe me."

The man turned with a swirl of his cape and walked towards the door. "I never forget a debt. Of that, you can be assured. But also be assured that should my existence become endangered in any way, I will do what is best for me." With that said the man was gone.

Lucius stared at the spot where the man had stood. "Of course, old friend. You are a god after all."

ABOUT THE AUTHOR

T.L. Shively is an award-winning author who plays mom and wife with a daytime job but after hours you will find her knee-deep in gnomes, fairies, and all things fantasy. She loves when her imagination takes her places she hasn't been, then she writes them down on paper so she can share them.